17th February 2025

To my multi-talented Grandson.

Rohan,

SANCTUARY

I hope you will remember my stories and remember also:

There is only one way to succeed in anything and that is to give it .... EVERYTHING!

Love you, love you love you,

Baba

x x x x x x x

SANCTUARY

BY PEEPAL TREE PRESS'
READERS & WRITERS GROUP

PEEPAL TREE

First published in Great Britain in 2024
Peepal Tree Press Ltd
17 King's Avenue
Leeds LS6 1QS
England

© 2024 Individual contributors
Jacob Ross

ISBN13:9781845235956

All rights reserved
No part of this publication may be
reproduced or transmitted in any form
without permission

CONTENTS

Dedication	9
Editor's Note	10
POETRY	9
Athira Unni	14
To Calicut	15
Along the Conolly Canal	16
Atlantis	17
Sheena Hussain	18
Returned	19
Poetry Library on the Fifth Floor	
of the Royal Festival Hall, For Hamja Ahsan	20
Sanctuary	21
Crafting	22
Sometimes	23
Samra Mayanja	25
On the tongue, through the teeth	26
The past was rich	27
Quake	28
Holding onto Excessive Language	29
Passing Grief	30
Peter Ejedewe	31
The Visit	32
Finding Uncle	37
Mango	38
Listen	39
Jazz	40
Janine Griffiths	41
Immaculate	42
Returned to Sender	43
Emily Zobel Marshall	44
Mardi Gras Under the Freeway	45
Quiet Stones	47

Siesta	48
All My Lovin	50
Made of Light	51
Lemons, tomorrow	52
House Martins	53
Left	54
Rheima Robinson	55
Appleton Court	56
Hopes and Fears	57
Protest	59
Rasta Love	60
Spencer Place	62
Ginalda Tavares-Manuel	63
La Luz	64
Dead and Wake	65
Chérie Battiste	66
Sistahood	67
The Portrait and the Frame	68
Three Coats and a Djembe Drum	70
Khadijah Ibrahiim	71
Veneration	72
Dispute	74
Comfort	75
Lara Rose	76
Dear Bunmi	77
Omolara	78
I know, I hear, I feel	79
Prayer	80
Geraldine Connor – a Civic Unveiling (November 2022)	81
A Yoruba incantation in Leeds	82
Lorraine Dixon	83
Brimham	84
Life	85
(Home) from (Home)	87

Musufing Whyles	89
She Who, Who She?	90
Omari Swanston - Jeffers	95
My Father's Son	96
Daddy-love	97
Natalie Anastasia Davies	98
Treading Water	99
Have you ever nearly drowned?	100
The echo of your name	101
Ndidi Nkwopara	102
Drowning	103
Buka Market	104
A Place to Hide	106
I Dance, You Clap (Lagos, Nigeria 1992)	107

NARRATIVE

Adam Lowe	111
Beauty, The Beast	
(Angela Carter Exquisite Corpse Cut-Up Mix)	112
Melody Walker	115
Red	116
Barsa Ray	133
People Like Us	134
Gloria Hanley	143
The Parsonage	144
Nana-Essi J. Casely-Hayford	149
The Antidote	150
Saluka Saul	156
Best Room Misadventures	157
Savitri Pema	164
Pebble on a Beach	165
Shani Alexander	173
At the funeral	174
Jason Allen-Paisant	178
A Different Kind of Play	179
Malika Booker	183
How Tiny Got Lucky	184

DEDICATION

Peepal Tree Press's Readers and Writers Group dedicates this anthology to two of our writers who sadly passed while we were putting the book together. Ginalda Tavares-Manuel was only in her mid-twenties when she died – all the more saddening because this writer had just begun her exciting poetic journey, unravelling the rich web of her African, Portuguese and Cape Verde heritage. Her poems are included in this anthology.

Yvonne Witter's passing was equally shocking. She was Interim Chief Executive of Operation Black Vote and a valued member of Leeds' cultural community. Part of her memoir-in-progress was published in our previous anthology, *Weighted Words*.

Peepal Tree Press's Readers and Writers group extend their profoundest condolences to families and friends.

EDITOR'S NOTE

Peepal Tree Press's Readers & Writers Group's second anthology of creative narrative and poetry is a satisfying confirmation of the value our participating writers have derived from their continued work with Peepal Tree Press.

Not only has the quality of the writing improved but, since the publication of our last anthology, *Weighted Words*, several of our members have appeared at public readings, have had their work published in anthologies and online magazines, and/or are currently developing more ambitious creative projects.

A couple have already distinguished themselves by having their books published: Emily Marshall's collection, *Bath of Herbs*, appeared earlier in 2023 with Peepal Tree Press and her second collection is currently under development. Gloria Hanley, the most senior member of the Readers and Writers Group, published her second memoir in October 2023.

We also welcome creative contributions from nationally profiled, award-winning Leeds-based authors who are closely allied to the Readers and Writers Group. They include Malika Booker, Adam Lowe and Jason Allen-Paisant.

One of the outstanding features of this anthology is the diversity of themes and styles, a testament to the remarkable growth of the group over the past two years. Contributors are pushing against the boundaries of the various forms they are engaged with. Their work is no less nuanced and introspective than the previous anthology; if anything, it is more daring and exploratory.

A feast of themes, styles, subject matter and insights awaits the reader: from frank and powerfully erotic fantasy to meditative interrogations of the writer's relationship with the physical spaces they occupy. The poems and stories seek to unravel the delicate threads of loneliness and longing, of the personal quest for a certain kind of reprieve from the relentlessness of life. A daughter dreams of another life while she cares for her elderly, declining mother; another records her restless poetic musings as a "Covid refugee". Yet another invokes that magical moment of stillness when a poem arrives.

The family features strongly here: a character seeks to uncover the secretiveness surrounding her birth in a family which looks so obviously different from her; a struggling housemaid finds her predicament mirrored in that of the mistress who has employed her. There's light and humour too: a woman finds an unusual way of dealing with her cheating partner's betrayal while two sisters bring a twist to the Caribbean tradition of keeping a parent's body in the "best room" before sending them off to their final place of rest.

It's all in here: bitter-sweet interrogations of fatherhood; fractured childhoods; the politics of love, redemption and abuse. The shocked awareness of a world turning on itself.

We'd like to believe that this is an anthology that you, the reader, will savour and enjoy.

Jacob Ross

POETRY

Athira Unni writes poetry and lives in Leeds. Her début collection, *Gaea and Other Poems* (2020) was published by the Writer's Workshop, India. Her poems have appeared in *Channel Magazine, New Note Poetry, Gulmohar Quarterly, Sheila-Na-Gig Inc., Sunflower Collective, Paper Dragon, The Alipore Post, Madras Courier*, and *NAME* magazine. Other writings were published in the Contemporary Women's Writing Association (CWWA) blog, Voices of Academia, MAP Bangalore (blog) and the University of Glasgow End of Life Studies blog. She is currently doing her PhD at Leeds Beckett University and working on her second book of poetry. She likes good coffee, art and thunderstorms.

TO CALICUT

Yet another misty shower waters the moors.
On the horizon, a church spire stings the sky.
Trampled grass under bovine commas –
brown, white, and black.

While sitting at my window
this lager-laden Yorkshire evening,
I imagine your friendly shores:
a beach stretches with kites –
numerous. I remember
the smell of pickled gooseberries,
acidic, the unhappening shore
with memories of short jaunty walks.

You wait with morsels of biriyani,
and sarbath, and muttamaala.
You inflate my heart gloriously
and re-member me
in one-word sonnet memories.

I remember you, dear town,
haunted by crows, and your colonial debris
of a sea bridge. A baby owl perches and hoots.
Nuns smile and sing hymns. I will return
for a chicken dish and a glass of lime tea.

ALONG THE CONOLLY CANAL

Atrophied water wires my house
to the bio-park. I creep out of bed,
paw my way out, to walk in the park.

The water is staid since 1848. I see you
waiting, with young melon-seed eyes.
We walk silently beside the fidgeting trees.

★

Now, I see woolly moss
bloom between cemented ground,
the old waste-den with shards
of bottles, now all cleaned up.
Mangroves reach out
like sailors in a shipwreck
under the shadow of a shark.

These neat cemented streets
watch the stupefied waters.

The canal runs halfway, my place to yours.
Will you come kiss me again in the park?

ATLANTIS

Through the plain glass window
I watched lightning strike the Empire State.

The city was a stork and I, the changeling,
as if Atlantis had never sunk
but shrunk and crept onto land
to emerge in time.

Everything multiplied in the city:
Chinese scarves, stocky buskers,
silver torties.

Ding-dong! "PIZZA!" The blue hat
rushed out stumbling on sealed letters
in the hallway, smelling of socks and coffee.

Through another window, I saw
a tired man sitting on the carpet
to play with his daughter.

★

Green/ Yellow/ Red lights over ground.
Busy faces/ voices/ paths underground.
On the pavement, a bouquet of heartbreak.

I wore floral print trousers
and felt like a Lilliputian on long walks.
Whale buildings walled the streets
of this island of ateliers,
rap battles and laundromats.

One evening, I stopped by an old church crouched
between megalodon jaws. It stood at rest
as the world spun in ballet shoes.

Sheena Hussain is a British Pakistani poet, essayist and cancer advocate from West Yorkshire. She's a non-practicing immigration lawyer who turned to poetry after receiving a cancer diagnosis. She's published a collection of poems titled, *Memories of a Poet, My Road My Recovery*. Her latest work includes "Poem: 99, Poems from a Competition". Sheena's work has been widely anthologised in publications such as *Porridge Magazine, Purse Slush, Truth Serum Press, Cambridge-Hall Poetry Journal, Samfiftyfour* and elsewhere. Her poem titled, "Watching a Green Fly", was longlisted for the Leeds Poetry Festival Competition, and "No Thanks" was shortlisted for the inaugural Curae Prize. She is also a carer to her mother. When she has time, Sheena enjoys climbing mountains.

RETURNED

You reached for your neighbour's hand. It is not like when you arrived in this City of Sanctuary. You saw the curve of your smile echoed in her welcoming arms, like the warmth from the kettle in your kitchen; the smell of freshly ground cardamom and hibiscus flower – sweet scents of Syrian centuries. You think of the curl of your husband's arms around the swell of your waist. Everyone, especially the old man, your neighbour, delighted in your labneh, drenched with golden oil and freshly chopped mint. Those were the carefree days. Now, you stand as white as your hijab, your face painted with terror. *Don't send us back.* You try, you try again; again you try. You cry. But there is no home now – no bustling house of merriment. You are led away to the deportation centre. They mean business. You have bidden farewell to your neighbour. And you wonder where your children are, if they are not at the edges of the sea, floating like life jackets.

POETRY LIBRARY ON THE FIFTH FLOOR
OF THE ROYAL FESTIVAL HALL

For Hamja Ahsan

Brother writes poetry
on the busts of women tattooed on walls.
He tames an entire poem in the circumference
of a one pence piece. Poetry is a kind
of contraband. Somehow, he gets away
with it and thrives whilst shut away in prison.
He has Asperger Syndrome.

I am the brother of a terrorist
in tabloids and breakfast time TV.
I tell myself it will pass – the long days in solitary
confinement and leg-shackled showers.
For a moment I could happily
take his place; his mind, his hands
become his stanzas.

The fifth floor of the Royal Festival Hall
is a library in exile. I am drawn to my
favourite spot; everyone here is an activist.
Logic is no longer logical. Here,
I make friends in the classroom;
some are more learned than I.
I keep it together
by the pull of prison poetry.

SANCTUARY

the glint of moon on sacred skin
a bowl of summer marble cherries
the ancestry I hold on to stronger than belief
the quiet repose of the encased mind
the mouth & bone of bird song
my childhood screams and laughter
the ascent of an impenetrable heart
the vine of a lived love story
the icy sip of raspberry tea
sitting in the niksen of nothingness
a loquacious book
the dawn dew beneath my feet
the call to worship and to fully submit
watching the walk of clustered clouds
that memory of you at first base
the seismic belief that I am and I can

CRAFTING

Somewhere in the ribs of this story, it is
okay to flow to the edges
free
       fall
within the pull of a projectile.

Today, twelve hours
in A&E, things do not change; pressure is
piling. Thoughts of losing a limb,
never hearing the dawn chorus again.
Imagine the day when the wisp of a breeze
is no longer there.
Here I am, crafting a way out.

SOMETIMES
For my beloved mother

My childhood head weeping. A tall terraced hallway
where windows wore bridal nets. This world, our home.
I was safe, in the curve of your belly.
That day, you returned from your usual trip to
Morrisons. Two bags. Weight of washing powder
in one and a jar of seedless jam in the other.

Perhaps I was meant to live in the stillness of your
adapted room. Watching you rock back & forth as if mourning
a death. It's not dementia but still the soulless pain has to
vacate somehow from the swell of your feet
neatly placed as if they were
a pair of shoes on the hard floor.

Perhaps today I will not
eat. Perhaps, I will sit in your presence.
Perhaps, my feet will force me to walk an inch or
two. Perhaps, I will open the window so you can smell
fresh air or speak to the indigo sky.
Perhaps I'll cry. I do cry.

Sometimes, holding hands bent like the beaks of birds
is enough. Sometimes I notice your
plait-end is dry as the pastry brush you haven't touched
in years. The stone, substitute for water.
The size of a milk top for *wudu* weighs you down.
Beneath dupatta, the smell of jasmine and ageing hair.

I rush to empty your commode.
I mustn't delay this.
I wonder, are you privy to
these small acts of duty
I love you more than our DNA.

Maybe you hear the cry I make to God
five times a day?

Sometimes, I ask,
why is she locked in when all her children
are outside of pain?
Perhaps it was fate that I share your pain. Sometimes,
I drown my patience in the reservoir you've never seen.
Perhaps, on occasions, it's for the best.

Samra Mayanja is an artist and poet who has exhibited, performed and lectured both nationally and internationally. Her practice emerges from the limits of art and writing, where the limits of each give life to the other.

ON THE TONGUE, THROUGH THE TEETH

We are a choir that sings
so the living, the dead
and the lost
can pass each other.
Our songs form a porous passage
that transport but never hold.
I'm part of a people that have always
sung the mourning song.
Our voices are the choir inside
flown in swooping murmurations.
Then I was dying.
We made chorus with the wind
that will someday whirl me away.

THE PAST WAS RICH

1.
Bradford: Everyone shouts here. Croaky thrusting
vocal thuds. Women beat men in the street,
vociferating, of course.
From opulent Victorian windows
we sit on the ledge of separate sockets,
hollowed out by industrial demise.
We daren't use the echo for company.
Barely kiss – we can't.

2.
Our toilet bowl is stained yellow now.
I keep cleaning it but new marks appear.
Do we need stronger bleach?
My alias is DUTTY_NITE
His is ALMOST_WITE
Our itchy carpets are sodden in patches
of piss topped with bleach.
It's hard to know who went first.

3.
Day 7 of the 10 day lockdown.
I'd prefer a "lock in", something fun
between layers of our king-size bed,
him asleep between duvet and quilt
me velcroed to the level below.

4.
Today we saw an African man
carved into a building called Sunrise House.
Palm treed and lust lit.
When I tried him on, he didn't fit
over bulky rivulets of fear.
Empire, I see us everywhere.

QUAKE

In the first chapters of Jennifer Nansubuga Makumbi's "Kintu", we learn about a Ganda custom where foreigners – anyone from outside – must forsake their names, culture and history for a Ganda identity.

Yanked from Sudan as soldiers,
we were rustled together by a series of quakes.
In Uganda, where everything is public,
we squabble, bathe and die in the street
in view of a past that cooks us
until we melt quietly into this landlocked pot.

HOLDING ONTO EXCESSIVE LANGUAGE

There were nights when we were grafted together
so tightly that it made us both disappear.

The shape of the hold:
lounged back into the body, ready to receive,
yet protected from the fullness of my weight,
you become a kind of headless recliner
with a two-pronged fork for legs
which allows a head to rest on a shoulder.
Latching on isn't just a rule,
it's our doctrine.
I'm thinking about your hunched solidity
and the choke-hold that is us,
since, the one who is held can only breathe
when the hands of the holder releases.

PASSING GRIEF

In my hand is a scrunched up note
from the one I am supposed to love.
It says:

*Untethered faces of the departed
inside a ball, smashing into walls
then unravelling in a slump.*

P.S - Missing the rasp of touch.

x

Peter Ejedewe is an English Course Leader at Leeds City College. He grew up in Leeds with Nigerian and Jamaican parents, from where he takes many of his writing influences. He is a graduate of Leeds Metropolitan, Huddersfield and Warwick Universities.

Peter came to teaching after he became disillusioned with the school experiences and achievement of Black students, and has just recently completed developing a Black British History curriculum. He is currently completing his MA at Leeds Beckett University. An avid Leeds United fan and lover of European culture, he enjoys film noir movies, reading fiction, collecting vinyl of original Coltrane and other jazz greats, and travelling to the Iberian Peninsula. Having lost his 95 year old father in 2023 – one of the first permanent Black residents in Leeds – Peter's writing has begun to draw on his Nigerian and Jamaican heritage.

THE VISIT

I was shocked when my parents decided to sell me.

Three months from my eighth birthday, a man came to visit from Nigeria. He was from my father's village, so that made him family.

Till then, our family was Mama, Father, my sister Sylvia – oh, and Snowy the cat, a stray that turned up at our house and stayed. Mama does nursing shifts at St James's Hospital. Father engineers in a steel works far away. Sylvia is eleven and always playing with dolls and brushing their hair. I have four action men, eighteen Matchbox cars and Mama says I read as well as most ten-year-olds.

We live in a three-bedroom, red-brick house on Sholebrook Avenue. The thirty-two houses on the street stare at each other across old cobbles, as if waiting to see which blinks first. Most have identical wooden gates in various colours. Some have brightly painted doors. Ours is blue with frosted glass and a knocker.

"Obina," my father says, "your Uncle Abe wants to take you back home to Nigeria with him. You are to be engaged."

A rush of superheated air invades my core.

My eyes focus on the intruder. His robes are sails around a mast of black marble; his arms are thick, knotted mahogany, with shells of beaded iron bands. He has the most astonishing face: taut, high cheekbones, wide flaring nose. An expression of fierce kindness radiates from him.

My mouth has gone dry and I am shaking.

Why are they getting him to take me away? Don't they love me anymore? What did I do?

"What's engaged mean?" I ask.

No answer.

I begin twisting a loose thread from my grey shorts, around my finger. My mind floods; my eyes fill.

Mama's voice pierces the thick air. "But you don't have to go!"

My shoulders drop. Nothing more to say then; panic over. It's near the end of the summer holidays. It is past lunchtime but Uncle Abe insists we go out to eat. Twenty minutes later, I'm watching the back of the intruder's head from the oven of Father's Jaguar. The polished leather smells like burnt cigarette ends. They velcro my legs to the seat. I'm squished between Momma and Sylvia.

The car rolls off smoothly as if on rails. I bore my eyes into the back of the man's head.

Father chats lightly, as if a bomb hasn't just exploded in the family. "So Bumi is a grandfather already, uh huh!"

I watch beads of sweat chase down his nape. He wriggles to loosen hot skin from the sizzling leather seat.

We pile into the "Caribbean Cabin" on Mexborough Avenue – a relief from the hot can of the car. The eatery is a waterhole in the community. Tropical yellows, greens, purple, ocean blues, coral pinks and gold assault the senses. The heady aromas of pimento, garlic, peppers tug at our noses.

Mix-tapes of reggae tunes wallpaper the 40-seater space. The bass thump of Mikey Dread and I-Roy sauce the snapper and rice 'n' peas. Father wrestles with the boiled dumpling in a rich brown beef stew.

A slow salute comes from the Hylton brothers, Ronnie and Rudie, eating with their parents. Rudie jumps to his feet but is stomped back into place by a large woman in a powerful leopard-patterned robe and head wrap.

A crescendo of Caribbean patois mixed with over-pronounced English makes me wobble with joy. My sister, Sylv, manages to slip away to her friends. Crouched beside them, she is pointing back to the table, at Uncle Abe.

"Where your Father comes from is about one hundred miles from Abuja," the stranger says.

I don't know where that is. I suck hard on the Ribena dregs from the carton.

What have I done wrong? I can be a better son.

I search the faces of the adults who are comfortably chatting away.

Back home, the tall visitor rises from the lounge chair. Once again, Father refers to him as "Uncle Abe". They cannot be real brothers. Father is an only child.

I observe this mountainous Uncle swaying like the sycamore tree down the lane. He wears colourful sheets masquerading as clothes. They come straight from the pages of the *Encyclopedia Africa* on the bookshelf in the best room. His hair is shaped like a dragon-blood tree, and splayed at the side like elephant ears above his strong neck. Each sandalled step is deliberate.

Sandals in Leeds! No socks, mind you; just bare, wide feet. A bit dry.

Mama excuses herself, pushing Sylvia ahead towards the kitchen. I still have questions.

I observe the dark stranger chatting in Yoruba. I know a few words like *Ek'Abo* which means "welcome"; *S'owadaada* "are you okay" but not *betrothed*. Father didn't want to teach me Yoruba because I was born in England.

I don't have to go. Mama said that. Or did I imagine it?

I cross my legs tightly; I need to pee, but I'm afraid I will miss something.

"What does 'betrothed' mean?"

My uncle looks down on me. Four scars gouge each cheek like deep-ploughed fields. They look angry and ancient. I mirror them over my own face with my fingers.

"Proposal, dowry and marriage!"

My jaw drops.

Father dips his head, peering over tortoise-shell rims. "I'm watching you!"

The stranger holds my gaze. Grown-ups barely notice me but the stranger sees all of me.

Be quiet, go to your room, come wash up these plates, do your homework, listen to your mother, get to bed... These were Father's only words to me in all of my seven years. Still, I value them. I watch them passing a tiny black and white photo between them. "Obina, come look at your fiancée!"

Fiancée! – another adult word I don't know.

A girl of four, maybe five, is sitting on a huge raffia throne. The photo is curling, going brown in the corners.

"You will marry this girl!"

Marry is what grownups do to have a family. I like the one I have.

"She's a baby. I'm not a baby. I won't –" I feel a long scream coming on.

The visitor snatches me up quickly. In seconds I am in his claws, facing him.

He places me astride his knees while Father nods slowly, as if he is agreeing to the kidnap.

The man's rich tones ripple around my head.

"In Kaduna State, you would be an honoured guest. You will live in a large house with servants. Your grandfather is Baba Ayinde Seye Mobo Adeteyo Ejededawe Oba."

All those names for one person? He's making this up.

Uncle inhales deeply. "For a boy of seven."

"I'm nearly eight!" I insist.

"Hmm, well for a young man of eight, let me see…"

He starts a story about a yellow sun that rises to kiss each cheek awake and stays the whole day; about sitting in the shade of sweet gmelia trees at midday. I imagined cool blue waters and elders humming hymns while young boys chase chickens and milk goats…

I must have fallen asleep. They are still talking when I wake. My uncle's ploughed scars are standing proud. Intricate and parallel patterns guide my eyes over his features. Was it from a lion's claws or the end of a branding iron? Father has no marks.

My fingers wander over ridges and deep ravines – a tapestry etched into mahogany flesh, like raised letters on a book cover.

"Does it hurt?" I ask.

Uncle Abe thunders as he pitches me over his knotted trunk. "No, I had these many years."

His English accent is warm, heavy and rich – as if deliberately basting his tongue with butter.

"Father, where are your marks like Abe?"
"Obina, eh! eh! Who are you calling Abe?" White porcelain gnash. He springs to his feet. "Show respect or..."
I recoil into Uncle's perfumed chest.
Uncle Abe sharply raises a large hand, freezing Father.
"Food ready!" Mama calls.
But we've only eaten a couple of hours ago.
We rise like a congregation, Father directing Uncle to the table.
"This looks beautiful Behula! Bless you!"
My brows furrow. I nudge Sylv. "Who's Behula?"
She nods at Mama.
My fork is stabbing into a crisp dumpling when Sylv nudges my elbow. "I'll miss you, Sprite."

FINDING UNCLE

I am empty,
weighed down by blind obedience.
I am a chasm parched of knowledge.
I need to drink.
O man,
douse me,
drown my curiosity.
I'm a bowing ostrich at the watering hole.
O Father, you left me thirsting.
O Uncle, you allowed me to grow in your soil.

MANGO

A rainbow palate lingers in a box of straws,
sixteen yellow eggs in a cool nest.
We bite down and sink into juicy pulp
like eating sticky sunshine,
we chomp chomp until porcelain smashes into stone.

LISTEN

Not silence
not quiet
not absence
not alone.
Steaming eucalyptus opens thoughts
spooned over truth.
Anxious eyes freeze on nights' ceiling.

Scent of melting traffic lingers on the evening breeze.
Streetlamps hum a lullaby to night.
Echoes of crying skies beat against the far-off mountains.
The stillness in dwellings broken by the cracks of aching hearts,
the music of lost souls settling.
Listen…

JAZZ

Like terracotta tiles melting across a monochrome chess board
skeins of liquefying smoke pour into a tall waterfall of whiskey.
A jaguar slumbers on the sultry shoulder of night
striding between midnight tears.
We traverse alleyways to smoky rooms of tense bodies
swimming in the loneliness of each note
that rises, catches light, pulls on our closed throats.
The poem of a lone trumpeter dances with ghosts
and a lazy bird falls in love again.

Janine Griffiths is a journalist, copywriter, and creative writer based in Leeds. She works as a freelance journalist for the BBC and has previously worked for the *Yorkshire Evening Post* and *Shropshire Star* newspapers, as well as two marketing agencies.

Beyond her journalistic endeavours, Janine extends her literary skills to the realm of playwriting and poetry, earning recognition in Chapel FM's *Missing* anthology. Her creative pursuits converge seamlessly with her other passions – travel, hiking, cultural studies, and a keen interest in politics. Her blog janinesjourneys.com, serves as a chronicle of her experiences navigating the world as a third-generation Caribbean woman.

Originally hailing from London, she has called West Yorkshire home since 2009, infusing her work with a unique perspective shaped by her diverse experiences and environments.

IMMACULATE

You painted your rooms in pastels,
each one a different colour,
immaculate and well presented.
Your kitchen was to die for.
I didn't see the emptiness at first.
Now we cannot even sit and talk.
Doctors come and go.
It is hard for me to stay.

The living room is silent.
The wooden floor is stained.
Boxes fill the bathroom
and jealous aunts who came and went
don't visit anymore.
These lemon walls now look decayed.
Trash lies on the floor.
Home is where the mind is;
that's a truth that I now know

RETURNED TO SENDER

Little girls are meant to love their mums
– an unwritten rule of life –
but my heart is numbed,
a deadbeat in my chest.
You see, I'd never learned
that love comes and goes
if it ever comes at all,
and maybe Mum is just too empty
to love a daughter like her own.

So, instead I smile and make pretend
while all the love I've ever posted
is returned to sender.

Emily Zobel Marshall is of French-Caribbean and British heritage and grew up in the mountains of Snowdonia in North Wales. She is a professor in Postcolonial Literature at Leeds Beckett University. She is an expert on the trickster figure in the folklore, oral cultures and literature of the African Diaspora and has published widely in these fields including her books, *Anansi's Journey: A Story of Jamaican Cultural Resistance* (2012) and *American Trickster: Trauma Tradition and Brer Rabbit* (2019).

Emily has published in the Peepal Tree Press anthology, *Weighted Words* (2021), in *Magma, Smoke Magazine, The Caribbean Writer* and *Stand*. Her poetry collection, *Bath of Herbs* was published by Peepal Tree Press in July 2023.

MARDI GRAS UNDER THE FREEWAY

As Miss Delphine steps out the door
she pauses. The sunlight skids up
from the sidewalk,
rests on her bright orange hand-stitched
Ankara dress, scatters across the wooden slats
to hit her beaded shoes
creating constellations.

On the steps of her porch, she feels the
drum-roll tremble,
the street-shake of
processions drowning out
the traffic-drone

The spirit grips her,
arches her back,
kicks her feet above her knees;
now she's spinning across
hurricane-split paving,
is dancing
the dance of Black skin worn thin,
now shining
in the blare of
brass and thumping drums.

She walks towards the dark of the underpass
and the segregating highway;
a trombone wail turns her liquid;
she hip-rolls –
her seventy-year-old body
tricking time as it follows
the pitching
rhythm of the band.
From this corner of the city

under the freeway,
she joins the call for freedom
with a fierceness so bright that
when Miss Delphine walks home that night
she knows the stars cannot shine
brighter than her people, or
the shimmer of
her dancing shoes.

QUIET STONES

Before you stride to squalling summits
towards altitude and views,
stay still.

Hear the quiet stones
on which you stand
shift though time.

Listen to songs of the trickling burn
stroke cushions of sandwort.
Watch galaxies of saxifrage
inhale bog myrtle's lime-green tang.
See how all that grows here
does so without fanfare.

Note how water droplets cling to stems,
slide and settle,
their globular domes
mirroring the dance of wind.

Stand calm as the dripping
heads of cotton-grass,
ghostly in the mist.

It is on the mountain slopes
and not on peaks
you'll find the rapture that you seek.

SIESTA

The forest sighs, relents, and wilts;
the baking earth sleeps.
Only the cicadas are busy
sawing the syrupy air
of this sweltering afternoon.

In the shuttered house, the family is
spread-eagled on beds and sofas,
limbs twisting damp sheets
in these fevered hours.

I long for the river,
to escape the thick-walled cloisters
of Mami's home.
I crave for it now as I did as a child
on stifling summer holidays,
Mum, Mami, Papi endlessly insisting
on the importance of siesta,
of staying still at home,
of sleep, enforced.

The fan strums thick air;
fat, heat-drugged black ants zig zag
up the whitewashed wall.
I lie on my back and dream
of the cool currents of the Gardon river,
of fingering the silt of crystalline
metamorphic rocks,
of the soft-mouthed feel of minnows
nibbling ankles,
of sinking to the riverbed
on current-smoothed stones,
of lying on my back and looking up
through the blurring flow to

the blazing blue,
of becoming algéed,
mud-mulched,
of becoming river.

In dreams, I float like this
while the earth blisters,
until evening and the promise of
fresh breezes starts to
unfold across a heat-struck
Cevennol sky.

ALL MY LOVIN

All my lovin... pipes through the car radio,
flooding me with an image of you both.
You're 1970s young and dancing, Dad in his
flared brown cords, biting his tongue because he's so
focused on staying groovy and coordinated.
Mum flows in a denim mini skirt,
strapless canary-yellow top, afro fluffed
and patent white boots hugging
young-girl legs.

He's never met anyone like her,
this dazzling Caribbean woman, BBC job, beauty and brains,
and he, she thinks, is enthralling – maybe a little on
the small side, but with full kissable lips and a head packed
with grand ideas.
Close your eyes and I'll kiss you
Tomorrow I will miss you...
They move their hips in tempo,
this striking mixed couple, while people watch
sipping drinks on a brown couch,
wondering where she's from
and how he pulled her.

Then my glimpse is gone
and I'm driving on a motorway again, in the rain,
but there it is, a knowing in my gut;
I was born of bold and different dreams.

MADE OF LIGHT

On this ocean
I swim outside time
outside fear
below the call of gulls
as the dim shadows of fish
glide beneath me

I am
the wash of currents at my thighs
I am
the cold pull at my breasts
I am
two circling arms
shattering
kaleidoscopic
sunbeams

I swim into the sun
eyes closed
fireworks flash
behind my eyelids

Now, I can reach
a horizon
suspended
for I am only ocean
only light

LEMONS, TOMORROW

Early December,
I walk a muddied footpath
along the river Wharfe
to forget your diagnosis.

And I remember the lemon trees
on that Greek island
after the rain:
citrine gems throwing fresh
antiseptic scents into sapphire skies,
mingling with the tang of goat dung.
Winter-ripened, crystal droplets
clinging to sunset rinds
perfume the breeze long after the
clear disk of the Spring moon
cut the ocean's skin.

Tomorrow, I will bring you lemons.
Grate and squeeze them, add amber honey,
a steaming bedside brew in an NHS mug.

You won't drink much,
but through throat and nose you'll travel
to a small Ionian Island, ripe with lemons after the rain,
a clean smell of hope
not hospitals.

HOUSE MARTINS

The house martins are busy
nesting in the eves,
sculpting mud ball homes;
their brood is late.

Silhouettes in September sunshine,
plucking flies from air,
they dart like arrows arching
across cobalt blue.

There is purpose in their industry
while I sit and write nothing,
pen resisting forward movement.
For me, only this emptiness exists.

Why can't I snatch syllables from air
and lay them onto empty pages?
Lately, I've been constrained from
soaring on the slipstream of my words.
Lately, my dreaming has been stemmed.

I will watch and wait
for the undamming of this heart.
When it breaks,
I will write about house martins,
whose brood is late.

LEFT

There are three of them,
tiny, coiled commas. Tender snouts
tucked into soft pink bellies,
spikes still yielding under fingers. Alone in long
allotment grass on a heat-blurred
summer's day.

My children scoop them into jumpers,
carry them home, careful as eggs.
House them in a paper-lined box,
see their petal tongues lap cool water,
invite the neighbours over
to watch and coo.

When I ask why, the RSPCA lady explains:
For 6 to 8 weeks, hoglets are fed by their mothers.
Disturb a nest, and she can abandon or eat her babies.
Sometimes a mother will leave the nest
for no discernible reason.

I think of the sun, of lost, dehydrating hoglets,
of an abandoning mother. Does she feel
the sharp ache of missing
that stills her in her busy hunt for worms?
Or does she live her self-filled days
unfettered by the drag of nests
and clinging babes?

Rheima Robinson is a poet and cultural producer. Born and raised in Leeds, Rheima started writing with Leeds Young Authors, a poetry and performance group. Since then, she has continued to write, perform, and facilitate workshops and events throughout Yorkshire and internationally. Rheima is the Founding Director of The Sunday Practise (TSP), a cultural hub providing opportunities to creatives.

She has appeared nationally and internationally as a poet, including at The Chicago Theatre, The Nuyorican Cafe (NYC), The Historic Hampton House (Miami), and the UK House of Lords. Her poetry can often be heard across different media outlets, including BBC Radio and BBC i-Player. She was one of the BBC's *Words First* 2020 finalists.

APPLETON COURT

It's the cigarette smoke
drifting through open windows.
It's the constant sound of construction –
the drilling, the hammering, the lad-laughs.
What is it that has been broken?

It's the unnerving look
and frightening rumble of the elevator;
the cheerless concrete,
the rectangular redbrick lumps
black-scrawled
like elementary drawings of Lucifer.

It's the pulsating fridge,
the flush of the upstairs neighbours' toilet,
the cascades of takeaway flyers through the letterbox,
the junkies hounding my buzzer for building access.
Everything is so loud.
What are they even fixing?
Is this my future in this vacuum?

Out there the windows are closed
like the eyes of dead souls.

I am exhausted, I look my age.
My neck is stiff, my back hurts.
It's hard to dream here,
so many doors stacked on each other.
I see slave ships;
I want to jump overboard.
My seasick thoughts
are crowded with limbs
of drowned bodies.
I cry into the ocean.

HOPES AND FEARS

So tired of being woken by the sun
I bought a pair of blackout curtains
and two pillows for the sofa.
The job of crawling into myself
does not pay very well.

I become my own prison guard
and scorn her authoritative footsteps,
melancholy glances as I pass the mirror.
She is my only company.

All the best and worst things
now merge into a mushy, mundane pot
of the new normal:
Netflix binges,
Homemade Biscoff Cheesecake,
Egusi in Costco containers…
Did I mention I bought new houseplants?
I fear they will die.

Zoom meetings.
Skype meetings.
Google meets.
Instagram Live.
YouTube Live.
I wash my hands.

Solitary Birthdays.
Pink Gin.
Amateur Yoga.
Chronic pain.
I fear I could die here.
I wash my hands.

Entanglements.
Petitions.
Fundraisers.
Black Lives Matter.
Did I mention I shaved my head?

I hope the sun stays.
The moon, the care,
the mercy, the love.
I hope for today, for many tomorrows
I hope that I'll still be here. Tomorrow.

PROTEST

I cannot tell you
about disorder,
about relentless cries,
of mothers whose sons
swallowed tear gas,
voices burnt
into waxy mumbles,
chambered
by the echo of
emptied barrels.

Smoke bombs
ignite the unrested spirit
like white sage
wavering under exploded noses.

I cannot tell you
about placards
curled and creased
like dried petals,
of "sorry-for-your-loss" bouquets
in the hands of daughters,
who will search for departed fathers and lovers.

I want to tell you
that there is so much existing to do
before, in-between
and after
consuming chocolate-dipped strawberries
or placards left on pavements
like an offering to a God not shared.

There is so much persisting to do,
so much undoing to do.

Between all the surviving,
there is so much living to do

RASTA LOVE

The love I had for him
would tear through tendons,
shred my logic to pieces,
all the control I thought I had
over myself and my emotions.

I wonder if he knows that I regret the loss
of almost all of our moments together?
I loved him and he knew it,
my bear, hairy bum and all,
no locs, but golden.
I would curl and shrivel
like a raisin; his eyes,
holy, kept me holding on
with every ounce of skin.
I want mine next to his
on top of his, inside of mine,
so he could love me to the fullest.
His eyelashes curled around my beauty,
my beauty in awe of his strength.
Traces of my love for him line my veins.
I think of how our attraction
was so innocent, untainted.
Then time aged us.

I miss his imperfect smile,
even the way he would disrespect my body
like he would disrespect his mother.
I want to resurrect our love.
I'd dare to play God for Adam
for the man of men
I & I
Ras of I
I would dare to play God
For the king of I.

SPENCER PLACE

My body moved under his breath.
Flickering, burnt out, scared of the dark,
I waited for the sun to rise.

There was a bible under the pillow,
small enough to fit into the palm of my hand,
too big for my cervix.
God never arrived that night

I lay still.
My insides did not.
Birds broke the silence.
Sunlight illuminated my shame.
Even so, I leaned into its warmth
and began my walk to the building which housed me.

I thought of my mother and his
– two women who would shame me –
like in the bible
which could not save me now.

Ginalda Tavares-Manuel was a Leeds born-and-bred language graduate in Spanish and Japanese. She spoke English, Portuguese and Crioulo – a native language from Cape Verde. She was a writer and poet with many interests. In describing herself she said, "I come from a place of broken homes, broken bellies, and unfinished business and postcode wars. I come from a place of fish and chip Fridays, Sunday stews, daily prayers, beans and fried plantains; leftover Cachupa com Ovo in the morning. I'm from a mixture of cultures that makes me, me." Ginalda died in 2024.

LA LUZ

And on the first day
the light was upon us.
Crack of dawn
birth of sun
rain of light,
my hair grows outwards and towards it.
It feeds my scalp,
nourishes my melanina.
La luz nos lleva –
we are lifted by the light.
Do you see us,
the way our shadows move?
Black bodies shining in grey cities like lanterns.
We are the luz that light the night.
Our incandescence is here to stay.

On the horizon,
hot sun swelters
on black bodies;
mountains call to me.
I can tell you my rituals:
water parting over my head,
body foamed and scrubbed at the hammam,
fresh skinned, new skinned. Healed.
Black is beautiful everywhere
I am my own sanctuary.
Each braid I embroider into my head
is a gesture toward sacredness.
I baptize myself with salty ocean water
I say: *Ase-o, obrigada, gracias, to madre mia*

DEAD AND WAKE

I
Sings Umbundo song – "Take my hand, God"

La Niña inglesa con sangre africana
Portugués, Angola, Cabo Verde
Su vida verde como la Arbola de la vida
Empieza suviaje en el tiempo.

She begins her travel through time,
her jet-black hair, free flowing,
pel the colour of espresso.
Corpo sinuous like the Okavango river.
These Umbundo women collect waters
in a river that has no end,
but this journey will one day find its Atlantic.

II
Kimbundu – a foreign language to my ears coz I was
brought up in England, Yorkshire –
but my ears tuned in,
it felt so familiar.
I reach for the leaves of the family tree.
Teach me, I say,
and they extend to greet me:
Your people were leaders, hunters and warriors.
Stories arrive and sit beside me.
There's a land called home and we're building on it, they say.
The walk is long but your *casa* is not far away.
You will be a part of it one day.

Chérie Battiste graduated from SOAS in African Studies, then worked in TV research on documentaries relating to Africa and the Diaspora. She moved onto acting, winning the Norman Beaton Fellowship and a contract with BBC RDC. She has facilitated creative workshops in prisons, PRUs and schools, and project-managed the embedding of creative learning in schools for Creative Partnerships.

She was published in the anthology, *Tangled Roots*, was included in the Saboteur Award-winning anthology, *Remembering Oluwale*, and her debut collection, *Lioness*, was launched at the Tetley. Race and identity feature strongly in her work. She explores her personal story of being transracially adopted.

SISTAHOOD

These friends
who are soft
places where
my spirit rests,
they see the scars
– all the places where,
like them,
I too have been broken
by the same tests.
They take my despair,
show me the hope in it –
the refracted light
of friendship

I have these friends
who are ego-eroders
patriarchy decoders
fellow female soldiers
who make
black power fists
with me.
We – women with iron-ore cores,
with causes forged in fire –
are sista-outsiders
still-we-risers
self-care silver liners
We are
preservers of an uneasy peace.

THE PORTRAIT AND THE FRAME

I want to look at this
portrait of you forever,
my original masterpiece.
I'll always lift and cradle you
because you're the portrait
and I, the frame.

Your voice is pitched for life's audience,
quoting phrases verbatim from Youtubers
through lips tired of waiting
for their stake in this day.

What makes your days
are codes trickier than Minecraft,
passwords for life
which I'm glad you don't yet know,
because in the sanctuary of Mum
it's all about swagger,
testing what it means to be a blagger
while learning new languages and new landscapes
in the safe harbour of me.

There's a new knowing that we're sharing;
here, no guns are blaring.
You clean out your hamster at midnight,
lit by a reading light,
claiming that you thought it would be alright
even after I'd said no more playing tonight.
Did you misunderstand me,
or are you pushing against boundaries?

As you turn, I see your cheeks rise
in a brazen smile;
this, I think, is where you start your own impala leap.

Your first walk to school alone
bouncing up the street,
and from me comes
the muffled, tearing sound
of slow umbilical release.

You say, "Bye Mum"
nonchalantly,
a bit too loud,
scanning for friends to see,
then lingering a while.

For now you're pushing borders
with skinny arms
that will one day thicken and open wide,
but I want to hold this picture of you forever
in which you remain the portrait
and I the frame.

THREE COATS AND A DJEMBE DRUM

Urban stark, rush-hour stalled traffic,
I stand static, djembe drum
cross-strapping me, burst bags flanking me.
I wear three coats undone,
see pity washing over drivers' faces.
In their floodlit glare,
I'm a dark girl lost in dark,
but a quiet elation flows through me.
No more nerve wracking
mind-hacking conciliatory talking,
I'm escaping his military tracking,
I'm hijacking his daily stalking,
I'm abandoning fear
and running clear.
I'll be my own safe house.

I weave across street-chaos to the station
deftly dip and dart
through the rip of rain,
slip between the moving trains.

I told him if he hit me again
I'd leave.
I left.

Khadijah Ibrahiim is a published poet, theatre-maker and interdisciplinary artist from Leeds with Jamaican roots. Her work has been featured on BBC 1 xtra, Radio 4 and Radio 3; in international university journals, poetry anthologies, galleries, and museums. Peepal Tree Press published her collection, *Another Crossing*, in 2014. She co-coordinates the Readers and Writers programme at Peepal Tree Press.

She's received numerous awards during her career including Leeds Black Award 2011 for outstanding contribution to arts, Leeds 2020 Legacy Awards for international impact on the arts and the Arts Council of England's Developing Your Creative Practice award.

Her work includes "Dead and Wake", "Sorrel & Black Cake", "Rewind & Come Again" and "Flying" – a reflection on contemporary life. She was the Assistant Director for the theatre production of *Nine Nights*; Director and Curator of *Steel Pan Stories* for the Performance Ensemble and Leeds Playhouse. In 2023, she was a Forward Poetry Prize judge. In 2024, she was elected a fellow of the Royal Society for Literature.

THE PICTURE LIBRARY 2022

(Commissioned poems, Leeds Arts Gallery)

Kokeshi Doll painting by Kaoru Kawano

Veneration

Sometimes we search/ for
shadows/of the past/the essence
of things
that seep
through wood

The recrudescence/transcends
quietness
of space
spirit tiptoes
between/ loss
hope or wealth

The seer who/ scrawls
the grain of age/
the hold of the womb
knows /the truth
of grief

Hears the whisper/ first
light/ releases flutes of Kokeshi.
Bows appear/ buried

as porous/colours slip inside/blood
red/ black /white tints

brush strokes/
resurrect/ a farewell gift

There is an afterlife that's carved
in wood
that is also ceremony and veneration

DISPUTE
(*Goan Woman* 1951 by Laxman Pai)

        Across the shores of discontent

a Goan woman carries yesterday's moon as
sunlight /to harness/
        the landscape /partitioned

like each breath.
Sounding / gut-turning bitter taste

Colonial conflict records
time

        an endless beat
        beneath the ground

she moves fiercely
her peppery
        steady feet size up disputes,
        knowing the dirt/ that makes

date palms
Flourish /
        To pronounce a stance
        Like the weight of freedom

and what is not said
is seen inside her eye

COMFORT

(*Comforts of Home 1985* by Karen Babayan)

Home comfort/ alter the space for
lamentation/ faith reveals

A mother cuts and clears daily troubles
from dawn to sunset/for a family feast/
prayers are uttered/for the dead

she prostrates five times a day
on the worn-out red patterned rug.

Hemmed in the sanctuary of her home
Weeps secrets
waiting /daily cleanse

Slow fingertips roll
99 beads for glory in an afterlife

to complete each day
untroubled by hunger
troubled by grief/ released by
the white threaded dawn.

Lara Rose is a Leeds visual artist, sculptor, poet, author, singer, and songwriter with roots in Yoruba culture. In March 2021, her poetry was published in the anthology, *Weighted Words* by Peepal Tree Press following her first book, *Victory the Other Side – 24 Simple Tips to Keep Going Daily*, published in 2016. Lara recently graduated from her PhD studies and was awarded the title of Dr. of Philosophy, creating the first life size sculpture of a black woman in Leeds, that of Dr Geraldine Connor.. Her research focuses on how Yoruba culture influences artistic practices in Leeds, including assemblage installation, sculpture, carnival, music production, Yoruba *oriki* (praise songs) and the role of wordplay. She coined the term "Afropolitan melodies" and "Afro Dada", fusing Yoruba and English languages and culture in her writing, musical and artistic practice.

Lara was also a part of Geraldine Connor's phantasmagorical *Carnival Messiah*, at Harewood House and Royal Albert Hall and is now a Creative Associate of the Geraldine Connor Foundation.

DEAR BUNMI

I've been trying to write this note to you, my 8 year old self.
I have many crumpled sheets torn from the pages of my mind.
Why did you think of killing yourself so young?
From a simple lesson learned in school:
grip two large rusty nails
one in each hand
plug them into a three-pronged socket.

And you, a shadow of a girl
trying to figure out a way to insert the third
– a trinity that would finish you –
your hands still unsteady
from the beating you'd just endured
naked, stripped,
whipped
with the long brown stick
purchased at the marketplace
at Oju Elegba Junction Roundabout –
Oju, the eye of Elegba
at the crossroads of Sabo and Yaba Market,
the market, now also a place of punishment.

I guess I deserved it after all.
"Don't take your toys when you go to play," he said.
I took my dolls to play next door.
The white one I left intact;
the black one whose hair I hated so much,
I deprived of her arms.
Suddenly, my mum shouts my name;
I quickly toss the nails under the bed.
I tell myself, Bunmi, we will do this at a better time.

OMOLARA

My name, Omolara,
Yoruba for "this child (omo) brings wealth".
Yet, my mother has never hugged me.

Others say,
Omo – this child
L'ara – belongs to us,
is part of our selves.
Yet, I do not feel part of any tribe.

When I arrived in Lagos,
my grandma, Yaba, named me Bunmi
Short for Olubunmi,
meaning God dishes out to me.

If I were a boy, I'd get my father's name.
Since I have inherited my mother's
I belong to her. Besides, who would want
to be called Olufolahan Oguntade?

I KNOW, I HEAR, I FEEL

Using this green #rememberoluwale pen
I write his hardship in Leeds,
the electroconvulsive shocks at High Royds Hospital.
This pen hesitates, the ink is jagged,
skipping bits of meaning. Truncates
the word "leaving". Resists.
Even the pen is speaking of his brokenness.
I give up now.
Oh David, the stowaway,
I understand why you wanted to escape
though no solace waited here.
I swap pens for one that writes #respect

PRAYER

Blank and silence – ah!
Alas, I fight the silence, to contemplate.
Arise, start from the Ankh, to speculate.
Amen Ra, descends again from the ancestral plane
Baba wa (Our Father) Olodumare, Olorun ancient of days.
Clear this confusion, Jesu Kristi, amin o
Jesus, Esu, Jeshua, omo (child of) Mary.
Amen o!

GERALDINE CONNOR — A CIVIC UNVEILING
(November 2022)

Lara Rose dedicates her life-size sculpture of Dr. Geraldine Connor – the very first sculpture of a Black person on public display in Leeds.

A Yoruba incantation in Leeds:

Esu gbaragbomo juba are, are…
Esu gbaragbomo juba
Yeyeyeye o Osun, Osun O Are mi Osunwa se kumere

Ella Andall cried at the back right stairwell of Yorkshire Playhouse, Leeds. Her voice crescendoed and resonated around the auditorium. That sounds, I thought, like Yoruba!

In what parallel universe is there Yoruba singing in Leeds, a Yorkshire city, on a cold autumn night? Yoruba was the language we were not allowed to speak at home or school in case it contaminated our English words.

In my first experience of Dr. Geraldine Connor's *Carnival Messiah* (1999), the seeds were sown for further inquiry into a once forbidden Yoruba culture and language. Following numerous conversations with "Mama G" as we called her, and on her discovering my Yoruba heritage, she said to me (2010), 'Child you need to tell your story, your Yoruba story in your art." At that precise moment, I felt that Geraldine was giving me permission to investigate my heritage. My quest to explore Yoruba culture began, albeit with great anxiety due to demonising narratives I still held onto about Yoruba spirituality.

Yet more and more aspects of my Yoruba culture seemed to influence my artistic practice, fuelling my desire to progress from my MA to PhD study.

I never in my wildest dreams – 10 years ago – imagined that I would be standing here today with a 1.7 metre Aworan

Sculpture to honour Geraldine with this Civic Unveiling Speech, far less pursuing PhD study.

The 2020 Black Lives Matter (BLM) protest equally highlighted for me the importance of celebrating our successes while recovering from the trauma of racism and carving out equitable futures in the diaspora. Again, during the Covid19 lockdown and after the BLM protests, Leeds City Council (2020), carried out a review of statues by public consultation. Fortunately, this didn't flag up any unsavoury or controversial statues of individuals linked directly to the slave trade.

However, it did show how the Leeds sculpture and statue stock is out of step with its diverse community and recommended that more can be done to support diversity and inclusion with regards to future choices about honouring individuals in Leeds.

It is great that Yoruba Masquerades have evolved to Carnival costumes and Leeds Carnival, thanks to founder Dr. Arthur France, MBE. In fitting with the ancient Yoruba Aworan sculpture practice, I began to ask questions such as: what about the prolific bronze sculptures unearthed in Ile Ife by Frobenius and Bascom, some of which are currently housed in the British Museum, London? Where are the equivalent sculptures and statues of pillars of the community created by artists today in the diaspora, and in this case Leeds? What is the effect on the psyche to continue to hold on to broken narratives about Yoruba culture? How does looking and seeing Iworan art based in the broken past compare with art based in Afropolitanism, imagined futures and Akanpo?

It is therefore with great humility and gratitude I present this life-size civic statue of Dr. Geraldine Connor. It is ultramarine blue, to represent Mama God, Mama blue earth, Yemoja, Olokun and Joy like playful waves of the Ocean.

Lorraine Dixon is a music teacher and a poet who enjoys sharing her work in print and in performance. She has read her work at Fire and Dust (Coventry) and for Writing on the Wall's Writers' Bloc (Liverpool). She uses her poetry to explore the multiple elements of her identity as a Northern Black British woman from Yorkshire of Jamaican heritage.

Lorraine Dixon has had poems published in a number of publications including the *Train River Poetry: Anthology Summer 2020* (Train River, 2020), *Geography is Irrelevant: poetry in isolation* (Stairwell Books, 2020) and *Where We Find Ourselves: Poems and Stories of Maps and Mapping from UK based Writers of the Global Majority* (Arachne Press, 2021).

BRIMHAM

                    ice-prey
              sand-blasted
      moor-bones
other-worldly
                        shapes
in this weather of stone.
   Eye-frames,
half remembered
            hollows formed
                by clambering
                      kestrel-perches
     and
sole-palms
of the
snot-eaters
seeking out c r a c k s
       of ancient forms
          like Adam's ale
              packing winter's knife.
    It is but
skilled bone-smith
who with
acidic
caresses
says, "Let me bless you,
          shape you   and
    love you
into form."

LIFE
after "The Fish" by Marianne Moore

i
always knew
that i'd never, ever produce life.
i'm reminded of shrewd
maiden aunts who inhabit shad-
y
corners, not
connected with Black womanity.
slavery taught us that.
work-horse, sow, soil...

in the white
room, curséd place, the bespectacled
white coat said we'd need
further investigation and
an
interven-
tion.
legs splayed, tears shed
resigned to
accept the medicine's inward thrust,
but what do doctors
know?
what do they not show
to folk?

the black and reticent
form
they got from
the forms to hide the sick medicine
that stops the eggs
kills the onyx flowers.

no
need to look
here for sable spoils,
for harvest home.
it seems seed and soil are sterile.

yet,
idiom
and syntax have bloomed from arid earth
– ballad, epic, sonnet –
i laboured long and hard for these.

(HOME) FROM (HOME)
"... *this is all part of my culture, but which culture is mine.*"
— Louise McStravick

Cast-iron belly fertile with flavour-filled promise
of spiced heat ready to tek mi back home,
to the time "before Mumma an' Puppa carry dem grip";
to the place "where ackee nah come outta tin"
and salt fish is not some cheap cut
like pollock which rhymes with bollock
that I certainly couldn't say as a chile or
mi would get one piece a lick from Mumma
for thinking mi is grown fool-fool gyal!
My words heavy with audacious gasp
would drop dead to the floor.

I remember my aunty inna her yard
down Spanish Town picking ackee
laced with venomous intent
set against bright green dress, bunched like
an unforgiving red and yellow fist on the tree,
colours echoing the open fruit she expertly picked
from the forest outside her kitchen.
I remember the knife as sharp as her tongue
freeing firm flesh from pod,
then gently neutering pink frilly kitty
and the potent black seeds which can terminate the strong!

A good ting mi aunty always knew which fruit nah kill we,
how to prepare it nice nice so that it would whet
the appetite and taste good good straight from the Dutch pot
with calaloo, green banana and salt fish mi get
from Coronation Market in Kingston that same morning.
I weaved through crowds a likkle too fast

wid mi grey just-land skin. I don't get the low low price despite
how I feel up, feel up di yam with it skin like one crocus bag
or grab up the dasheen knowingly,
ready to drop inna mi aunty Saturday soup.

I smell the guinep, like an expert, careful to keep
the stainy juice away from my cotton frock.
But all mi hear is "Foreign buy mi wiers!
Look pon mi nice pumpkin, a only fifty a pound.
Luk pon mi garlic, mi tomato dem! Good fi Inglish eeh?!"
The vendor dem know mi is fram ova dehsoh,
like the guy in the continental shop ova yasoh.
He wants to get me on side to buy 'im wares from (home)
to fill my bag hanging empty like a craving mouth.
Makes me feel at (home), he calling out
in my heart language, "We noh only sell Tropical Sun, mi lady!"

Now, I walk the aisles of multi-coloured cans that take me back
(home) to mi aunty yaad and what kyaan grow
in an Inglish garden.

"Country roads take me home, to the place where I belong
West Jamaica, my ol' momma, take me home country roads!"

Yes, tek mi (home), whilst I nyam the salt fish an' ackee mi get
up real real early to make fresh from a tin inna mi kitchen.

Musufing Whyles is passionate about culture, arts, history and folklore and these interests form the backbone of most of her works. Born in the UK with parents from Jamaica, her Jamaican-influenced cultural upbringing keeps her anchored and provide a rich sense of belonging.

Her arts background and practice encompass theatre, writing and performance poetry, voice acting, podcasting, radio broadcasting, and production.

Musufing was commissioned for a Hidden Histories' arts project in 2021 for Assembly House Leeds where she wrote "The Bitter Tale of the Great British Sweet Shop", presenting the hidden and usually un-linked atrocities of the 17th century Caribbean and African cane sugar industry, that seminally contributed to building Britain's wealth.

SHE WHO, WHO SHE?

Mmmmhmm...
She, who dream her young gyal dream fi travel far fram up coconut tree hills and down cerussi bush gullies, where outside cooking fire smoke rise above de lush trees, an everybody get a taste a fry fish and bammi from country woman who keep her secret tight an shove her higgla money in de bank betwixt her breasts.

De dream of better tings fi come – and better must come – as de distant soun of Ska riddim-an-blues tune "Manny O" by Higgs an Wilson, drifts from a rum bar wooden speaker box. Daydreams of Englan turn reality! Ticket buy and ship deh at the wharfe.

"Oh Manny O, Oh Manny O, why did you go, why did you go? You leave me all alone baby, please come home"

Mmmmmhmm...
She, who get a rude awakening as she sit down pan the edge of a wooden chair at a cracked greasy plastic table in a brukdown cold Englan house where her man live with ten or twenty fellow-Caribbean man.

Her suitcase still by her foot, she hear de unfamiliar sound of de rubble a drop from de coalman sending coal down de chute to the cellar. She hold on tight to her peepee as she a wonder, "What is DISS?!!!" How she a go manage again to tek herself through the dirty backyard a watch her breath a blow before her inna de ice cold, fi go to de outside toilet?!

She call pan Jesus de Nazarene, she caall pan her granny, she cry fi her daddy who sell some of im best hog to raise her fare fi come a foreign. She quinge up, and finally accept, just like her peepee, dis England life she chose has to flow.

Mmmhmmm...
She who batta out her babies dem one by one, and sometime a two baby wrap up warm in de perambulator as she a dodge what de dog left on the pavement, a wheel her babies to pick up a milk token fram de post office.

She buy yam, potato, carrot, flour, salt mackerel and a tin o Milo. She feed an settle down de children. Nappy, uniform an shirt fi rub out inna de back wash room.

She thank God, because if it wasn't for de Trinidadian lady roun de kaarna who keep her baby dem, how she could keep de likkle factory job?

Her man finally reach home, dinner cook, paraffin lamp light, baby dem wash, cream, powder, an a sleep. She sit down fi de first time since she reach home with a hot cup a ginger tea and a needle and thread to mend a small pile of clothes.

Mmmhmmmm...
She go down a de school when de dyam dirty renk Mrs Winterbottom tell her son dat he "must've been raised by baboons in the jungle" because he did rough up one bwoy in de playground. Winterbottom never was there though, when de feisty white boy fling stone in her pickney headside an call him "blackie" so yes, a rough him rough de bwoy.

Winterbottom also didn't know her man told each of his children, "No badda better come back here fi tell me seh any baddi hit yu, caa, who lik fuss mus cyan tek lik, awwoah!"

She rushed from work de day to go a de school fi attend meeting with headmaster and when she left him office an im not looking, she served Mrs Winterbottom such a hot pepper sauce!

Mmmhmmm…
She, who realise that de Green Shield Stamp book ting was a dyam waste a time! Englan good fi show off pretty iron stove and electric blanket fi tek away people money!

She always pay her Empire Stores catalogue, wid her two job, even when her worthless neighbour beg her fi order one Kenwood mixer and only give her half de money, a she pay off de rest!

She find de pickney dem with the catalogue a laugh and point pan de white man dem in the men's underwear section a stand up, hand pan hip a model inna dem bumpy briefs and boxer shorts. She tell dem to behave and put down her tings.

She never miss a pardna hand, not like de worthless neighbour who she no chat to again (since she pay fi de Kenwood mixer) an she an aar man never yet haffi hide an screetchi behind curtain from NOT ONE rent man!!

Mmmhmmm…
She, who scrub out, den scaall her tea cup at work wid HAAT water every day an every day bleach-blonde Lorraine laugh at she, "Bloody hell, you an your tea cup, a bit a tea stain caah kill ya, love!" but Lorraine no hear the Jamaican proverb, "no mek one donkey choke yu!" She smile an scrub out the cup same way.

She who clean, wipe, dust and mop for miles, she could never count fi mek Englan a better, cleaner place.

Sometimes while she a work, her mind drift back to days when sun dance on her skin and when guinep season come and de sweetniss juss a roll round yu mouth wid de seed. She catch herself, an push the broom.

Then, some feisty white ones, sometimes the supervisor, even co-worker like herself, remind her wid scorn, wid dem actions and wid dem eyes, seh she black, like she no know! But a so de Englan tings go. She mek de sacrifice already and leave her birth-land fi mek a family yasso, so she do what she have to.

Mmmhmm...
She, who love a Jim Reeves of a Sunday when peas a bubble, she keep her household together, all her laangulala pickney dem, everybaddi hav dem chores and dem role.

Dem seh "Idle jackass go a poun" but not disya woman. She straang nuh box cyart! Because after all, a good and virtuous woman is a credit to her household. Even when not a soul but Jesus a look, when she a bawl down inna her chest, while she a beat peppercorn and pimento inna de mortar, because she never get fi bury her daddy back home,

becaaz all de work dem a work tings still haard,

becaaz aar man laugh at she: "A weh yu need new frock fa, when yu no have nowhere fi go."

Becaaz de young, slim, milk-coffee Island gyal smiling back inna de mirror gone to faart.

Becaaz her knee start bother her,

Becaaz she see her daughter hide with her white school friends round de corner when she sight her mum walking in her work clothes.

Becaaz a long time she no eat a GOOD mango.

Jus as one tear slipp inna de mortar, she swallow de pains

back down an beat de pepper and pimento in time to Jim Reeves. "There will be peace in the valley for me some day, there will be peace in the valley for me oh Lord I pray"

Mmmhmmm!

Omari Swanston-Jeffers is a multidisciplinary artist and educator specialising in dance, directing and literature. Dance is his first art form. Omari started his professional training at 13 with RJC Dance, studying West-African, Afro-Caribbean and Contemporary dance. His directing career began with the Leeds Playhouse in 2015. And *Northern Noir*, his first theatre production, premiered to sold-out audiences In January 2019. Omari holds a First Class BA in Creative Writing and a Master's in Education. As an educator, he's served as a high school English teacher for 5 years and has led an array of creative education workshops since the age of 16. Omari's art spans many genres from screen to stage to dance floor, from song to poetry. Nevertheless, as a published poet, the poetic form shapes everything. Today, Omari's work has no bounds. His art centres the stories of Caribbean and African Diaspora peoples all while shining light on their identities.

MY FATHER'S SON

Sat here in midnight November
inky cold hour
candle burning
incense smoking
jasmine tea cooling
music playin'

"Paula, ain't he mami
a Fitzroy?"
rolls off Grandma's tongue.
"You are your father."
"I'll never be like him,
with all his woman
after woman," I say.
But the other day
I found myself
in heated discussion
with a woman in a bar
– Marley, Jimi &
the Beatles plastering
the walls.
She has embers in her
eyes, gives me the 1-2, 1-2
with a sweet lipstick-sharp,
cut-blood smile
my skin in her gaze.
I am lake ice,
cool on the surface,
underneath, a dichotomy of
red lust and tendrils of fear.

I *am* my father's son

DADDY-LOVE

I see you everywhere
in the faces of the children I teach,
in the sway of brown skin,
in the beats and the basslines
Bashment Afro-Brazilian Favela Funk, Neo-Soul,
UKG, Newskool, Afro-British, Jazz Roots, Rock Steady,
Reggae and the blue hues of my people.
Will you look like me?
Will you share my skin, my full lips,
Granddad's chocolate nose button?
Your hair thick, natty, plentiful?
Your eyes lying low like mine, dreaming...?

Will you be blood-marooned – your skin
a mix of pimento velvet rum
gooseberry honey-gold?
Will you be laid back like your grandfather,
sing Lovers, Rock Steady, Soul like my mother?
Will incense-lit love soothe our home?

In my mind,
I hold your head on my chest,
tiny ears against my ticking heart
like my dad did me –
and so much more
and so much more.
I have not yet met you
and still I miss you
for all the love I have to give.

Natalie Anastasia Davies is a Northern poet and creative facilitator of Grenadian descent. Her work draws on themes of connection and memory, cultural identity and the global climate crisis. She uses experimental techniques to explore nature and wellbeing with developing writers and communities. It is her vision to draw parallels between the personal and global experience, to provoke environmental change.

Natalie was commissioned as a New Northern Poet by Ilkley Literature Festival in 2022 and has performed with Leeds Playhouse, Black Voices Matter and Apples and Snakes. In 2024, she was appointed Writer in Residence at Brimham Rocks by the National Trust and Word Up North. Her widely celebrated residency was featured in the *Guardian* and on the BBC news.

TREADING WATER

We walk in parallels
communicate across winds;
disturbed voices carry to hollow places.

Sodden, we mouth to ears
across moors. Heaved words fail
to breach the bleak distance.

When the body succumbs
to the onslaught, all that is left
is to hold the ground.

Somewhere in the quiet, I once read
that water-logged toes and fingertips
only wrinkle to grip the surface.

What is left when numbed fingers fail to grasp?
What is left when earth becomes reed and water?
What will become of us when there is no land left to tread?

HAVE YOU EVER NEARLY DROWNED?

One day your country will sink
into the gulf of warmed, unforgiving seas,
waters which false gods stirred into rising.

You will clutch onto boats and turn in turmoil
to safer lands which home dark tongues –
holding the body of your last born child.

And we "the safe" will watch from the comfort of land and say,
"Leave them. We cannot bear the weight of foreign beggars."
Whoever should try to save them will drown with them too.

You… foreigner
will beg until your throat aches with grief.
No gargled morsel of salt will soothe you.

Inches from death, you will be hauled
from the blackened ocean,
and grasped by a sheaf of shadowed faces.

In your despair, you will be branded criminal,
and only then from the churning depths of self-pity
will you fathom the meaning of refuge.

THE ECHO OF YOUR NAME

As we speak,
only dust falls, never settling
in the spaces between us.

Mahogany murmurs, touch
upon midnight, its edges
as indistinct as our own.

In the corner of a lamp-lit room
there is no sin-scorched sheet,
only solace in open arms.

As I surrender into your chest,
I remember the bass notes of a womb song,
the hum of a not so distant God,
remnants of forgotten prayer.

There is something in the skin,
soft and waiting. If love is worship –
might I be gathered, into heaven's arms?

Ndidi Nkwopara is an emerging creative producer of Nigerian heritage, based in Leeds. She has written two non-fiction books: *Retreat to Rebirth – My Story* (2019) and *Poverty is a Woman, Her Daughters Look Like Her* (2021). Her work focuses on themes that educate, re-orient and empower people to avoid emotional, financial, and physical trauma. She was the lead artist on Co-creations projects titled, "Creative Stories in Suitcases & Camera", and "Our City, Our Lives, Our Stories" for the Leeds 2023 Year of Culture. Ndidi is the Creative Producer of the Leeds International African Arts Festival (LIAAF).

DROWNING

He told me the god I saw was him;
I folded myself at his feet.
He's bone of my bones, I thought,
though he wasn't missing a rib.
His sides were filled with stones
that bruised me every time;
his eyes were never on me.

Oh! When the curtains fell,
the god I saw was Agbero,
throbbing with righteous anger.
I stood, rag in hand, beside
the gleaming surfaces of our house,
my apron reeking of spicy cooking.
Still, I kept the dust of the harmattan outside,
swept away the dried leaves at our door.
I held back the wind,
but the red rage that constricted his heart
found release through fists and kicks.
Now I know
I was a beached whale drowning.

BUKA MARKET

On the street below,
they grab bag-hugging shoppers from all directions.
"Brother, come and buy o!"
"Sister, open my market for me na!"
"Dadee! Dadee! Find something for your boys!"
"Your pikin go better pass us".

It's a hopscotch dance
between the yellow and black commuter buses
that drop off passengers in your face,
while okadas thread in and out of traffic lanes,
and fuming cars – the big, the small, the posh, the old,
the Tokunbos!

Shoes trip and dip into blocked gutters,
the busy air foul with bargain hunters,
starving beggars, street evangelists,
herbalists and industrialists.

This is Broad Street, the heart of Lagos City.
Hustle or die!

The rumble in my belly drags me along the potholed roads.
I surrender to the pull of stew –
blended and fried peppers tatashe
atarodo and shombo.
I'm urged on to Ghana High,
and the sizzling heart of Onikan –
a litter of Bukas –
a holes-in-the-wall heaven of food-stalls
that answer to names like
Iya Basirat, Wosilat, Sikirat, Alata,
where long wooden paddles dip and rise with
the stirring and the cursing:

"Shaki, Beef Bokoto, Kpomo & Roundabout" –
all parts of a slaughtered cow
spluttering in cast-iron pots
sitting squat on tripods
over smouldering firewood.

Each Buka boasts 10 cast-iron pots
lined up like grey, fat-bellied old men
grumbling their lives away.

I stand in line to order my amala.
In a charcoal-blackened corner
a pair of angry rats screech and claw.
Their strategy works.
A wave of disgust, followed by a lump of amala
folded in okra soup lands on them.
"Winch! Rat no de fear person again!"
Weariness envelops me and licks the flap to seal me in.

A PLACE TO HIDE.

Outside is black and shivering with mosquitoes.
Mugs of hazelnut-flavoured coffee sit empty.
In the solitude of the night,
I scribble and type.
A tale unfolds
becomes a place to hide.

Adrenaline pumps against the
deadline on my mind!
Whispers spool,
"Who sent you? You too do!"

I persevere
hit the "send" button
My poem becomes a wish.

I DANCE, YOU CLAP
(Lagos, Nigeria 1992)

"Mstchew..." She kissed her teeth again and readjusted the Vivian Bennett throw pillow. She shifted her hips beside him, closing the inches between them.

From the corner of his eyes, he observed her listlessness – another bad day at work. She regarded her boss as an ogre and the situation left her frustrated and powerless.

"Mstchew..."

He let down his CNN mask – that look of concentration that his wife and kids knew well. They knew not to bother him when he was listening to CNN. The news was all gloom and doom anyway. He turned to her; the corners of her mouth were turned down, her pursed lips tight. Next, she would be crying, regurgitating painful memories which she couldn't see was a self-administered poison to her soul. Tonight she wouldn't sleep.

As a psychotherapist, he knew the long-term effect of misery: raised blood pressure, increased heart rate and feelings of inadequacy, fuelling the need to belong, the impulse to compete with Brazilian or Indian hair, platform or stiletto heels despite the leg and back pain they caused her. Not to mention the gleaming gold jewellery – the chunkier, the more glamorous the better – and thick-layered foundation drawing brown maps on her collars. There were the bright red lipsticks their mothers didn't let them wear because they were not "ashawo". All of it, an unconscious rigmarole of denying the presence of your inner demons. Aah!

He came back to the present, flipped the channels and clicked on Chop & Clean Mouth's video, "I Cannot Come and Kee Myself". In a minute, they were in stitches, heads thrown back, legs shaking, laughing belly-laughter. Then the moment passed.

She stood up smiling and headed towards the hallway. "Let me check the kids," she said.

Na lie, he thought, I am not missing this chance. In one leap, he swung his legs over the three-seater leather couch and was behind her. He clasped her waist, nuzzling her neck and whispered in his baritone voice, "Don't worry, the kids are okay. Baby, check me."

"Chike!" She tilted her neck and giggled, then pressed his hands closer to her bosom. And with their bellies pressed together, they danced their earthly dance.

NARRATIVE

Adam Lowe is a writer, educator, publisher and performer from Leeds, though he currently lives and studies in Manchester. Adam has taught at the University of Leeds and the University of Central Lancashire, and has worked with The Poetry School and English PEN. He was named one of the "20 best writers under 40" in Leeds for the LS13 Awards and his chapbook, *Precocious*, was a reader nomination for the Guardian First Book Prize. He was a finalist for the Venture Poetry Awards, Eric Hoffer Award and Lambda Literary Awards, and was selected as one of 10 advanced poets for The Complete Works II programme, where he was mentored by Next Generation poet, Patience Agbabi. He is also an Obsidian alumnus. His first full length poetry collection, *Patterflash*, (Peepal Tree Press, 2023) was a Poetry Book Society Recommendation for Summer 2023. The book was completed as a result of Obsidian. He is currently studying for a PhD in poetry at the University of Manchester.

BEAUTY, THE BEAST
(Angela Carter Exquisite Corpse Cut-Up Mix)

1.

My monster comes to me, drenched in marbling moonlight, his face, a latticework of scars hooded by night. He always comes in darkness, limping through corridors towards me. I spend daytimes among an army of clockwork servants that meet my every need and desire.

His hands are hairy, his nails jagged. I smile, unnoticed in the darkness. I am in chains today. But this is what I want; this is what I bargained for.

As he approaches, he stinks. Urine-stained fur, dried sweat, the stench of carnivorous teeth. His swollen chest bursts through his frayed silk shirt and his claws click and clack as he crosses the varnished floor towards my bed. Beneath me, the sheets are stained with blood. I won't let the servants clean them just yet.

I am ready for him. He jerks my hair back, baring my jugular as though he might rip my throat out. The fierce hair of his chin scratches me. Claws run over my breasts, shredding lace and velvet, baring them to his sticky, panting breath. Against my leg, I feel his ripening cock, veined and hard. I coil my fingers in the tangle of his pubic hair and tug him towards me. His mane falls about my neck and shoulders, and I feel his heat.

He paws my stockings, tearing them away from my legs, and slides four fingers upwards, beneath my skirts. Pulling away my garters, he clasps my sex in his leathery palms and feels my nipples harden against his chest. As I lie back, he drops his trousers and straddles me. My beast-man hisses as I slide my penis inside him. My eyes glint; my mouth waters. Outside, a cloud covers the moon, throwing us into gauzy shadow, and my beast bleeds across the bed covers.

2.
Come closer, Beast. Put your matte paw here on my pussy. Ripple your fur and I'll ripple mine. We'll move like moonbeams in the night. Let me kiss you. I'll bite your furry throat. Turn around, as I untuck my pussy, unfold my balls, let the penis swing back into place. See me. Look at me. Do you like the stem, the balls, the weight? Now it's your turn. I'll make you a pussy too. On your front. Yes. Do you like that? Good. I can hear you panting. I can hear you purr.

#

Beast, you belong here now. You belong to me. Your feline tongue has lost its human words. Take mine. Listen to me. Now. Crawl through your shit for me. Let me lick your pelt clean.

#

Your smell is my smell. Your breath steady as a pendulum as we lie on this threadbare sofa. Empty cigarette packets torn open on the floor. Streaks of ash in your fur like old age, like smoky wisdom.

#

You won't move. My pussy prince, velvet boots kicked across the room – you lie like a sleeping lion. Your breaths throb slowly over leathery lips that barely twitch when I kiss you. Have I kissed you too much? Have I sucked away your life?

#

The bedsit stinks. Flies have made a mockery of our makeshift bed. I take the garden shears and trim you. I want to bare your skin. Have you lie naked beside me. You are warm again now. For a while you were cold. But the rats and the mice and all the writhing sons of that bluebottle army have breathed a sulphurous kind of life into you; have filled you with their sighing odes and pitiful adoration.

I hunker down beside you and nestle in. I feel your new life on my skin. I wear your furs. We are exquisite. I am Venus.

Melody Walker is a writer of the local history book, *A Journey Through Our History: The Story of the Jamaican People in Leeds*. She has also written extensively on a range of social, cultural and genders issues. Her short memoir, "Strands", was published in the anthology *Weighted Words* (2021). She also produced a short documentary, *Strangers with Blood Ties: The Story of Caribbean Child Migrants*.

Melody has a BA (Hons) from University of the West Indies, an MA and Postgraduate Certificate from the University of Leeds and Postgraduate Diploma from Leeds Beckett. Melody currently works as Head of Business Development for a Leeds-based national arts organisation. She was a 2021 Arts and Fundraising Professional Fellow through Cause 4 and the University of Leeds. She also provides capacity building and fundraising support for a range of charitable and voluntary organisations. A committed community volunteer and social activist, Melody remains an enthusiastic Philomath. She enjoys reading and believes that the last 20 years has marked a golden period for literature and films from people belonging to the global majority.

RED

Lavern walked steadily across the grilled veranda. Her neon-coloured flip-flops made a loud clopping sound in time with the sloshing hot sorrel tea in the enamel mug. She knocked softly on the door, waiting for Grams to grunt – a sign for her to enter.

It was her self-appointed duty to wake up her 98-year-old grandmother, Griselda Smith, with a cup of bush tea to help assuage her endless list of ailments. When she walked into Grams's room, she was greeted each morning by a peculiar sight. Through the slit of the drawn dark curtains, the sun beamed a spotlight on her grandmother's face, caked in full make up. Overnight, her face had slipped from glamour to frightful ghostliness. Lavern never got used to it. But Grams said she wanted to be ready to meet her Maker whenever he came for her. Every night, she went to bed expecting to die in her sleep and would wake the next morning disappointed that the Lord had not taken her. She'd been doing this since Lavern's brother, Robbie, went off to university while Lavern was still in high school in 1980. When it was Lavern's turn to go off to University in Kingston, Grams had told her that she wouldn't be seeing her again. She said the same thing through theatrical tears when Lavern left for her four years of study to England. Now, fifteen years later, her imminent demise was a soap opera playing on repeat in their household.

Lavern set the mug down and opened the curtains. She gently wiped the lumpy waste from Grams's face with a damp wash cloth. She wanted Grams to talk to her. Lavern needed Grams to help her resolve a puzzle that had been bothering her for the past two weeks and gauge her mood. It concerned her mother, Dolly Bailey. Her behaviour was becoming increasingly odd. Every time she tried to discuss it, Grams was seized by a sudden onset of sickness. This evasiveness made Lavern suspicious and she couldn't shake off this uneasy feeling.

Lavern had sat up most of last night on the veranda, looking out at the shroud of stillness before her, with billions of stars breaking through the darkness overhead. She'd listened to the night: its whispers, the undecipherable hissing, buzzing vocabulary of night insects. She'd wondered if they were talking to the ghosts that lurked in the bushes – the same ghosts that often walked in and out of her dreams. Screaming, jabbering ghosts; crying – always crying; rummaging around her mind in search of something that had been lost.

And now, it was as if the ghosts in Lavern's dreams were haunting her mother too.

Located below their hillside house, beyond the procession of ackee, banana and breadfruit trees and the stooping rows of herbs and ground provisions, separated by a stonewall, was a burial plot where four generations of their family were interred. Weary-looking gravestones bore the names of deceased McCleods and Smiths.

Dolly had become preoccupied with five stony mounds that sheltered under a barren cherry tree. When Lavern's grandfather was alive, he'd considered cutting down that wretched tree.

"You want to turn Dolly into a madwoman?" Grams had screamed at him.

Lavern was nine years old at the time and couldn't understand why a barren cherry tree would drive anyone mad. She couldn't bring herself to eat cherries after that.

At first, her mother would sit under the infertile cherry tree and stare at the mounds. Then one day, she got the yard man, Tall Man, to clear up the weeds covering them. Next, she had him cement them over until they looked like mini shrines.

Lavern had asked Dolly what she was doing.

"Red!" she snapped. "Do I ask you why you have three good-good degrees and sit down at my yard turning worthless. Hmm?"

Lavern had bristled at the use of her childhood nickname, Red – and winced as her mother's sharp words jabbed her in the chest. Grams, who was listening to her morning radio play, *Naseberry Street*, grunted reproachfully.

Dolly kissed her teeth dismissively. "The government spend a whole heap-a money to give you a scholarship to a top university in England and you come home and sit down like you no have no ambition."

Dolly picked up the cutlass and pan she was searching for, then marched down the hill and resumed working alongside Tall Man.

Ruffled, Lavern turned to Grams. "But Grams, what is wrong with –"

Grams put a finger to her lips and said cryptically: "Peacock hide him foot when him hear 'bout him tail. Red, that's how yuh mother is. Leave har." She went back to listening to the radio.

Lavern hated her nickname: Red. She'd been told that when she emerged from her mother's womb looking like she'd been lifted from a sea of bauxite waste, Rex, her father, had asked Dolly to wash the child again just in case her insides were still stuck to the baby. Red's colour was a source of contention between them. Two dark-skinned people shouldn't produce a child with hair and skin the colour of ripe coffee berries. Her older brother, Robbie, was a deep rich chocolate, so Lavern was teased mercilessly at primary school for being different from him.

Lavern had overheard her Great Aunt Mertle gossiping that her father had disappeared for months after she was born. For Lavern, red was more than a colour; it was a memory of unspoken hurt. Did her father think she was a jacket? Dolly wasn't the kind of woman who cheated. Rex was the cheating one, with a whole other family down in Discovery Bay. That woman had given him four children. Dolly gave him two.

It was during her teenage years that her complexion became a currency in the cultural politics of beauty and desirability. But the scars were already etched on her brittling self-esteem. Lavern had approached her father about her concerns. Rex, a quiet man, remote but amenable, looked at Dolly and Tall Man working away at the mounds. He shook his head and muttered:

"Dolly, what de hell you doin'?"

He had patted Lavern on her shoulder wishing her good luck and disappeared down the driveway.

After Lavern washed and settled Grams, she tried once more to broach the question about Dolly's mounds and her growing agitation. Grams brushed Lavern away, spilling some of her tea onto the floor. Frustrated, Lavern called the domestic help to wipe up the crimson puddle threatening to stain the tiles, and stormed out of the house.

Lavern walked up the road slowly. The weight of her worries felt heavier than the bags of fruits and provisions she dragged up the hill with her. The fierce morning sun, against a washed-out blue sky, was hot on her back, pressing her further into the asphalt. Her red, dreadlocked hair stuck to the back of her white camisole, her legs damp under her black jeans shorts.

She barely mumbled good morning to the passersby whose strained expressions of personal worries brightened briefly to sing out a cheerful "good morning". Those hustling to work – the anxious market higglers, the late hotel shift workers, and the sauntering farmers and coalmen swinging their machetes – would usually greet her decorously. But not the never-go-find-work, the-proudly-lazy and the-wait-for-foreign-money, they'd purr brazenly, "Empress!" "Red Nubian!", "Browning!" "My Queen!" Their eyes would linger over her body, stopping abruptly at the crown of her sun-burnt locs.

Lavern turned into the lush dark green pathway to her Great Aunt Mertle's property. The trees and shrubs were so high, they seemed to push the sun to the other corner of the sky. She welcomed the coolness as she climbed the steps of her grandmother's half-sister's house. Hibiscus flowers punctuated the dense greenness. They were not the light pink ones on the hedges at Lavern's family home, but dark and bloodied.

Great Aunt Mertle's dementia had made her into a whole new person. Foul-mouthed, and irreverent, she spoke rotten truths and lashed out with damaging delusions. Lavern would find her sitting on the veranda with her son, Glen, whom she no longer recognised. Frail from a stroke at the age of 69, Glen looked exhausted. Aunt Mertle was again yelling at him to leave her yard. She thought he was a lodger who owed her six months rent and she wanted him out of her place.

"You keep forgetting he's your son, y'nuh," Lavern told her, handing Glen the bag of goods she brought for them.

"My son!" Aunt Mertle said scornfully. "No sah, me no 'ave no son look so. Him look like su'ppen not even john crow want to eat."

Glen coughed, got up and dragged himself to his room. Lavern knew his mother's words had hurt him.

"Come Aunt Mertle. Get up. Lemme give you a bath."

"I look dirty to you?"

"Yes, Aunty. You smell real bad."

"Is the dry up su'ppen between yuh legs smell bad."

"Aunty! Wash out your mouth!"

"After yuh wash the red Rasta rat's nest on top of yuh head."

She was tired of telling them she wasn't a Rastafarian; that she was wearing Sistah-locs to express her pride in her African heritage. But that just made her family and friends wonder even more why a nice-looking girl like her would deliberately spoil her looks.

Lavern was Aunt Mertle's only visitor these days, aside from a young distant cousin who came by to clean and cook. Her church sisters and pastor would not visit her after she spoke of the pastor's indiscretions with women in the church and his many outside children. Enraged, the pastor rebuked her for being possessed by demonic forces and attempted an exorcism. But Aunt Mertle just threw up on his clean suit and smiled toothlessly at the embarrassed Pastor who pronounced her a "lost soul".

Aunt Mertle wasn't always a "lost soul". She used to be a successful shopkeeper with her own general goods and food store in the nearby village, Canoe Pond. It was nothing compared to the chain of shops owned by Grams and her best friend, Miss Lou, up and down Northwest St Mary. Grams and Mertle were half-sisters – same father but different mother. They were blood but had never been close friends. Lavern saw pictures of Grams's young adult life: Grams and Lou smiling in the foreground and a scowling Mertle always in the background.

The village called Aunt Mertle's place, "The Dead House". Her daughter, Natalie, died of breast cancer. Her other son, Nigel, had gone to Cayman and never came back. Her husband died of testicular cancer. Her father, a subsistence farmer, died beside his pickaxe in his backyard. And her mother – a lay midwife and healer – passed fretfully in her sleep. Lavern thought that Aunt Mertle's house wasn't so much haunted by the dead as being a place that bore the traumas of the living.

While combing her Great Aunt's hair, Lavern filled Mertle in on what was happening at home with Dolly. She could pour her heart out now because Aunt Mertle wouldn't remember a word of what she said. She told Mertle about Dolly's obsession with the five mounds, and her concern for her mother's sanity.

"Five graves for five lost souls," her great aunt murmured, a memory rising from a pit of darkness.

"Graves?" Lavern said. "They really small, y'nuh! No one could be buried there."

"The Lord never show Dolly mercy. Dead come after dead until you born –."

"What?" Lavern frowned.

Mertle poked her fingers into Lavern's navel. "You have chil'ren yet? I hope you not a cemetery too, eh."

Lavern pulled away from Aunt Mertle's touch. She straightened up to leave. Did she see a flash of spite in the old woman, or was it the disorderliness of dementia?

Glen shuffled into the sitting room and snapped, "Mum!"

Mertle's cloudy eyes blazed with rage, "Tell that tiefing man, I'm not his madda!"

The rest of her attack was swallowed up by a wet violent cough.

Lavern made her way up, then down another set of hills in Stewart Mount. It was rare for her to leave Aunt Mertle's house in a foul mood, not even when Mertle spewed obscenities at her. It was where she felt she was needed. She switched the remaining bag from one hand to the next. Five mounds! Five graves! Five lost souls! What Aunt Mertle was suggesting was not what she'd been expecting. They could be only animal graves, Lavern reasoned. For pets, perhaps? Pet cemetery? Really, Lavern? She expelled a soft laugh.

"Wha' sweet you so, beautiful?" The unmistakable voice of "The Anaconda", Jeffery Andrews broke her rumination. Lavern responded with a mock vomit. Whenever their paths crossed, The Anaconda would sing loud, lascivious comments at her.

"Pepsi Cola bottle shape/ Come whine pon dis."

"Length an' girth baby/ Gal, you no ready fi de Anaconda yet!"

He would grab himself and stick out his tongue, emboldened by her silent embarrassment. But today was not the day to suffer Lucifer's serpent.

When The Anaconda teased her for what felt like the 100th time, that "her batty flat like Tastee Patty" and "she no got no bumpa, but it's a good t'ing she cute", Lavern marched up to his gate: "Yes, mi no got no bumpa, because I'm not a car!"

Surprised at her response, he recovered quickly and laughed. "The mawga H'english lady have big chat today. Go gain weight on the bumpa and them chicken foot. Take some alum. The Anaconda need something to hold pon." He adjusted his saggy nuts loose under his shorts.

Lavern glared at his self-satisfied grin, a missing incisor on the left side. His eyes still crusty from last night's sleep, dancing. His chest rising heavily, exhaling his fetid morning breath. He had one hand on his growing tumescence, the other rubbing his hairless chest.

With the swiftness of a mongoose, Lavern dropped her bag, picked up a large stone and sent it hurling towards The Anaconda. The stone connected with his nose and left a leaking gash. Lavern grabbed her bag and sprinted towards Charmaine's house.

Yelling something about England making her mad, The Anaconda slammed the peeling white banister door off its hinges, leaving a pale red handprint on it.

★

Lavern always felt peaceful sitting under the tamarind tree at Charmaine's house. Situated at the highest point in Stewart Mount, they had a panoramic view of the village. Lavern could spot the top of Aunt Mertle's roof peeping through the crush of trees. She saw her family house against the hillside, the farmland around it and the graveyard. Her mother and Tall Man were like busy little ants around the mounds.

When Lavern's family re-located to the village when she was a teenager, she and Charmaine had become close. Charmaine was the only person who could call her Red and the word stung less. On her lips, Red cemented their blood ties, their unstated sisterly bond. The time they spent together was mostly in silence, eating mangoes, naseberries and the rare star-apples. Charmaine was the primary school teacher at the Stewart Mount school. She lived with her housebound father who was 100 years old. Her mother had passed twenty-three years ago. Her three brothers and sisters were scattered across North America. Charmaine never seemed to carry the burden of existential longings and wants. She was unmarried, without child, young, unworried and unshackled. Lavern came to feed off this energy, hoping to divine how someone could find happiness in such stillness, such silence and monotony.

She arrived back home and waved at her mother and Tall Man in the distance. Tall Man waved and smiled. Her mother stared back, arms akimbo, ignoring the salutation. Lavern knew that Dolly had been disappointed in her when she returned from England with dreadlocks and the gloom of the London winter skies as her only mood.

Before that, her brother, Robbie, had gone to UWI in Trinidad & Tobago to study mechanical engineering but dropped out before he completed his last exam. No amount of begging him to go back to finish his degree worked. They had sussed, through Rex, that a Dougla Trini girl had broken Robbie's heart and there was no going back to the island of his pain.

Dolly didn't show any patience for her children's angst. "You don't know problems yet. Did you have to carry water buckets on yuh head to bathe and cook, before yuh could go to school? You'd to walk six miles to school? You'd to bathe a river an' wash your clothes there? You ever go to bed hungry? None of you know real hard life."

"Neither did you!" Lavern threw back once.

"You and your brother have a better education than me and yuh father. We invested everything in all ah your education. What you all doing with it? Robbie ah waste him life, say him a medicine man, a her-ba-list... ah grow all sorts of bush an' a tell people how to cure sickness. Him a doctor now?" she asked scornfully, widening her eyes. "You children are ungrateful wretches!"

Lavern turned to walk away.

"Lavern Donette Ann-Marie Bailey! Clearly something's bothering you since you come back, and you not saying a thing to nobody."

Lavern knew her mother was fearful for her. Dolly lamented that everyone knew England turn black people mad.

"What those white people put in the water over there?" she'd asked. "They always taking something from us, and now they take my daughter's mind. It really no good for black people to stay in white people country long."

Lavern wondered if it had something to do with a man called Franklyn Buchanan who Dolly, Grams, Mertle and Lou always told stories about that made them laugh hysterically.

Franklyn Buchanan had gone to England to fight in World War I for King and Country and stayed until they declared war with Germany in 1939. With an RAF pension and a limp, Franklyn came back with a comical accent, and wearing a three-piece suit, top hat and cane in the hot sun. On Empire Day and the King's birthday, he would swap the suit for a faded RAF uniform, decorated with several unexplained medals, and then march up and down the dusty dirt roads to the beat of the villagers' mocking laughter. They nicknamed him Sir Franklyn, self-appointed Governor General of his own British colony. The name stuck until the day he died from heart failure when Jamaica declared Independence from the British Crown.

Lavern's grey mood was no laughing matter to her mother. Dolly had always approached life with emotional and practical efficiency – that was how her mother ran the household and raised them. She never had time for self-pity. She didn't wallow in her mistakes or dwell on bad luck. Dolly's idea of a pep talk was to declare that "Moodiness is an enemy of progress". "My children are too sensitive. They head soft bad. Them never get it from my side of the family. Only a soft-head man would pick up himself and have a whole other family in Discovery Bay."

So, their failures were their father's fault? Rex was an excellent provider – in many ways, a good father, she and Robbie agreed, but they both acknowledged he was a less than excellent husband to their mother. Her mother had efficiently compartmentalised her husband's second family. She'd convinced Rex to sell the house in St Ann's Bay and move to Stewart Mount on her family property. If she took him further away from Discovery Bay, then maybe her family of two children would stand a chance. Her mother belonged to a culture of defiant wives who didn't divorce their cheating husbands, just to deny the side chicks their dream of a fairytale ending.

Dolly had knocked down Grams's ramshackle house, replaced it with a four-bedroom and put enormous effort into becoming a partner in her own pharmacy. Had this been her way of avoiding the gossips and shame – and bottling her rage over Rex's infidelity? But why the war with her children? Why the fuss over the unmarked mounds?

Lavern was climbing the steps to the veranda to check on her grandmother when she bumped into Robbie. He shook the keys of her battered VW bug at her – the one she'd bought with the savings from her scholarship money. He had borrowed the car because his pickup was being repaired.

Lavern took the keys from him. "Robbie, what's going on with Mommy?"

"Oh, you no hear?" Robbie drawled. "Discovery Bay matey pregnant again. Baby number five."

"Jesus! At his age? Poor Mommy. Wha' wrong with Daddy? Dibby dibby!"

She would have words with her father when he came home, but now she went in search of her mother, filled with pity and compassion. As she walked across the yard towards the graveside, she saw a huge, newly built cross standing over the five mounds. It was painted in a loud red.

Later, Lavern sat at the table having dinner with her mother and grandmother. The competing smells of the roasted breadfruit and pickled mackerel were the only conversation in the air. Lavern broke the silence.

"Mommy? You put up a cross and paint it red? Why?"
"So?"
"You call me Red."
"Not everything's about you."
"You could've painted it white."
"It is the colour of the blood of Jesus Christ!"
Lavern scoffed in isbelief. "Is this about Daddy?"
"Lavern!" Grams interrupted. "Not at the table. Clearly, something is bothering Mommy and she's not saying anything to anyone."

Dolly froze, hearing her own words thrown at her by Lavern. They glared at each other, waiting for the other to pounce first.

"Red, stop! You can't siddown pon cow back and a cuss cow skin," barked Grams.
"Huh?"
"Stop being ungrateful in yuh mother house!"
Dolly made a loud sound in agreement.
"And you," Grams turned to Dolly, "Ephesians 6 verse 4 says 'Parents don't provoke your children but bring them up in the training and instructions of the Lord'."

Lavern knew her mother was trying to tell them something. Was it about her? Was it her father? Sometimes Dolly expressed herself not in words, but in wily, calculated codes. When she wanted to push Robbie to complete his degree, she'd invited everyone with a broken-down vehicle to leave it on their property for him to fix – her way of forcing him to see his true calling.

Lavern contemplated what the red cross meant. Red – the colour of blood. We are covered in it at birth. It is what runs through the veins of the living. It's the end when it spills out of us. It is the colour of our family's chaos – the colour of our dysfunction. What did it mean for herself, the fire-coloured daughter who stood out in a family of dark brown and cool mahogany? What did it mean for Daddy's outside, unborn child?

The ringing phone jolted Lavern into the moment. She got up and answered it. It was Glen. She slammed down the phone. She shouted at Grams and her mother that she was going to take Aunt Mertle to the hospital. Her mother got up to offer help.

"Stay with Grams," Lavern said. "Let Robbie know where I am going. Ask him if he can meet me there."

★

Lavern sat with Aunt Mertle in the shared ward at the understaffed Port Maria Hospital. One doctor and a few nurses were on duty. Lavern prattled on to Mertle in the spaces between the old woman's short naps and groans. She talked to her great aunt about England, her lecturers there, her friends, and the men she'd dated. Mertle drifted in and out of lucidity. She was sharp as a tack one minute, and then, like a Rubik's cube, would cycle through a puzzling range of identities. Aunt Mertle kept inserting fragments of a story between Lavern's pauses, to which Lavern paid little attention until she realised that Mertle was speaking about a "red child" and a young couple who planned to have a big family. Her words came in fragments and short bursts… The woman had taken more than two years to get pregnant before she had a boychild. Got pregnant again, gave birth to a stillborn. Six years and five still births… the whisperings about her womb being a cemetery… the woman's fear of being abandoned by her husband. The sixth child was a living baby girl. Mertle spoke of a nurse who took the child away and returned disturbed. Bad news, she'd said. The child hadn't survived. The distraught mother of the dead child had cried herself to sleep. There was a woman in the same ward, young, restless, weeping not for a dead child but for a living infant – terrified of having this newborn. So, she left her baby beside the grieving mother and ran. The next morning, the mother woke up with a red, newborn baby beside her. Realising the newborn's mother had gone, she packed up her belongings and sat with the child on the hospital grounds waiting for her husband to pick her up. They celebrated their new child, but there were too many questions and whispers about the child's redness from him and others. She told her husband the truth. That red baby was the beginning of the woman's crosses with her husband – but she wouldn't give up the child.

Aunt Mertle's clammy hands tightened around Lavern's. Lavern yanked her hand away, roughly; the warm, comforting sentiments gone, replaced by emotions she could not name.

*

Outside, warm rain slapped her face. It was three in the morning and still no Robbie. Her head was pounding. She had to pass on the news to Glen and the rest of the family that Aunt Mertle had crossed over. Could she tell them Aunt Mertle had left behind a sorrow greater than the pain of her passing?

Lavern drove home in a daze. Rain sliced down bitterly. A crooked one-eyed moon strained to see through the cataracts of dark heavy clouds. She sped bumpily past the roaring sea, its foam breaching the barriers and crashing onto the road. Lavern's bug spluttered, jolted and came to a stop. The little car had had enough. Where the hell was Robbie?

The night pressed against the car urgently squeezing a memory closer to the surface. She was back in England; it was a wet cold night. They were travelling on the M1 back to London, after a Freddy McGregor concert in Manchester. Everyone in Ludolf's rented car was high on music or substance. She couldn't recall exactly at what point Ludolf fell asleep at the wheel. The bone-shaking crash against the side barriers woke her up. A terrible pain in her abdomen kept her awake during the rush to the hospital. The doctor said something about a torn pedunculated fibroid and damage to her uterus. She would probably never have children, he said. He didn't look at her. He might as well have spoken to the bedside table. Not the end of the world, he'd added. You'll be fine. The warm brown eyes of the Kittitian nurse, contrasted with the doctor's indifferent steely blue, comforted her.

Lavern sat in the broken-down car and cried for the times she hadn't allowed herself to cry. She cried for Dolly who had to swallow her grief, and for the woman who left her in her mother's arms. She cried for the five mounds, the red cross and the family of women and men to whom she had been tied to all her life by love, but not by blood. She cried for her father's new outside child and for all the unformed children that would never find a place in the warmth of her own insides. She cried because she couldn't tell Dolly or Grams why she felt the world had suddenly closed in on her like a heavy velvet drape and would not lift.

She had been trying to uncover a secret within her family when she was the secret – a barren cherry tree of dry branches that connected them in pieces, not whole limbs that bore fruits. Their secret was that she had been plucked from another tree wrapped in a bright red bow and given away – a gift from another woman's garden.

It took her a while to see Robbie's worried face as he pounded on the car window, trying to pull her door open.

The sun had burnt away the darkness. Before her lay a scene of devastation: cracked windscreen, broken tree branches, saltwater tributaries running through the potholed street. Lavern stirred. She felt the stickiness between her thighs. Her cycle after the accident in England had become as unpredictable as her depressive moods. It would disappear for months and then reappear without warning. No tender breasts. No cramps. A scarlet flood of depleted hope.

★

Lavern stayed long enough to attend Aunt Mertle's funeral before moving to Kingston to kotch with her friend Trixie-Ann until she got on her feet. Before she left, Rex had guiltily removed Dolly's red cross, but Lavern got Tall Man to re-erect it. She painted the name, Lavern Bailey, in white on it, and the date 6 March 1966. Her birth date and the blood child's death date.

★

It is 2001 and a large crowd is gathered for Grams's burial in the family plot. She lived for 105 years. Lavern, teary-eyed, stands by the graveside with her husband, a light-skinned Afro-Chinese man. She is now a lecturer at UWI, her husband a dentist. Between them is their 2-year-old child, Rachel, who takes in the scene with an innocent curiosity that illuminates her beautiful coal-black face. The funeral-goers look from child to mother, father to child; their eyes asking unanswered questions. Robbie stands next to Lavern, his gentle hand on her shoulder; he runs a chain of car parts stores but remains a herbalist.

Lavern lingers as the crowd disperses to the repast. She watches Dolly and Rex walk away with Rachel, each holding one of her hands and marvels at how she looks like the daughter they should have had. But she is Lavern's as much as Lavern is theirs. Their family had settled on an uneasy peace. Dolly has stuck with Rex, bound by their losses and grief.

Rex had often driven to Kingston to see Lavern with care packages from her mother when she started speaking to them again. Robbie was always there to hold her together. Maybe one day she will search for the woman whose heart wasn't big enough to accommodate her, but whose head knew what was right for her child. She, Lavern, will always be a bisecting crack that runs down the middle of their family portrait, disturbing the bloodline. But this is the only family she knows and when her time comes, she wants to be buried here among the shrine of mounds and the faded cross, under the red hibiscuses that have long replaced the dead cherry tree.

Barsa Ray's short stories have been published in *Mslexia*, *Weighted Words* (Peepal Tree Press), *Present Tense* (Dahlia Press), and *Demos Rising* (Fly On the Wall Press). Her poetry publications include in *Filigree* (Peepal Tree Press), *Magma*, and *Skearzines*. She has been listed in Fish, TLC Pen Factor, Northern Writers' Award and elsewhere. She has an MA in Creative Writing from the University of Leeds.

PEOPLE LIKE US

Rich girls get married in silk. My wedding sari is cotton. But its red colour ignites my dreams for my new life. My friends are jealous because I am going with my husband to Bhubaneswar, the state capital. In our village there is one big man, the Jamidaar, who owns all the land. In Bhubaneswar everyone is a big man.

Bhubaneswar is five hours by road. I think we are early, but we have to elbow our way onto the bus at six in the morning. There is only standing room between people, luggage and chickens. The bus conductor shouts at everyone to put their luggage on the roof, but that only makes people hug their bundles tighter. The few passengers who have battered cases held together with twine sit on them rather than be separated from their possessions. By the time the bus sets off two hours later, it needs its own rope to stop it bursting at the seams. It sways and lurches but everyone is safe amongst the cushion of other bodies packed around them. Some people sleep standing, their heads nodding on their chests like pumpkins. I start to giggle at the sight but when my husband, Rama, fixes me with a look, I pull my sari odhana over my forehead and lower my eyes.

Dirt roads winding between banyan, peepal and mango trees, broaden to potholed tarmac which in turn become concrete roads with not a tree in sight. The rice paddies have vanished under houses and stone-crushing factories. Before the sound of the wedding ululations have faded from my ears, they've been replaced with the honks of city traffic. The air dances ahead of us.

Rama rents a hut in a slum whose tin roofs are as low as the soaring apartment complexes opposite are high. A thirty-foot road cuts between the two sides like the blade of a sword. Rama gets work as a day labourer. I knock on doors in the flats across the road. Most times a maid answers who tells me the Babu Ma don't need anyone else, they have her;

then shuts the door quick. Sometimes the Ma of the house answers and grumbles about her maid who bunks off ten days a month. I tell her I have worked in the house of the jamidaar in our village. That I never missed work and was especially trusted with washing the china and the silk saris. I get three jobs in one week.

As I go about my new neighbourhood, I start recognising the faces of some of the maids who shut me out. We walk together to the flats each morning. They ask where I'm from, who I've left behind. Even the ones who've lost their jobs to me toss their heads. "There are other jobs," they say, because they want me to cover for them when they fall ill or visit their villages.

When our son, Tulu, is born, Rama and I are happy. So it must be fate. I don't know if he misses his people back home or whether it is that bunch of men he sees in the evenings, but Rama takes to the bottle. I cajole and beg, then threaten and cry. Then I get used to it. My husband becomes a shadow. I hardly see him in the daytime. He comes home late at night when I'm half asleep, exhausted from sweeping, mopping, washing dirty dishes and clothes for thirty people. He is breathing, moving, looking, but nothing of the world touches him.

Tonight he comes home in a stupor and refuses the food I put in front of him. He collapses on the floor and is dead to the world. I watch him for ten minutes but he doesn't stir. I cover him and go to sleep. Nothing I haven't seen before. When I wake in the middle of the night he's shaking, like he is possessed. I grab his arms and he is burning up. Then I see how yellow his skin is. How had I not noticed before? I press down on him with all my weight but I can't stop his fit.

I run to Sanju Maa's flat, on the top floor of the second apartment block. I ring the bell and pound the door until her husband Amit Babu answers. "Bhagya! What's the matter?"

"Please… please come, Babu! Tulu's father!"

I am crying and then Sanju Maa is holding me, saying

something. My mind doesn't grasp the words but I look at her kind face, the high forehead of the well-born. Focusing my attention on each of her features calms me down. By the time we get to my house, Tulu is awake and Rama is still.

"Can you hear me? Look, Sanju Maa is here. And Amit Babu. Wake up!" I shake him.

I can feel his heart beat under my fingers, thank God! Little by little, he opens his eyes. I heat up some milk which he drinks. I can feel Tulu's eyes on the glass. He will have to go without in the morning.

"Have you been drinking again? That cheap hooch?" Amit Babu says. Even this late his kurta-pyjama are without a single crease, not a hair out of place, and he sees everything from behind his gold-rimmed glasses.

Rama shakes his head. At least he has the decency not to look in Babu's eyes. I am so ashamed.

"Have you no care for your wife and child?"

Sanju Maa touches Amit Babu on the arm. "Let him sleep now. We'll take him to the hospital in the morning."

Babu flicks a glance at her and she falls silent. I hope her offer to help hasn't put him out.

Amit Babu drives us. I hope Rama doesn't throw up on their seats. I can't believe that people like them are driving us. It's saved me a hundred rupees.

The doctor on duty says there are no beds and points to a spot in the corridor. "Why do you people waste our time, anyway? As if we don't have enough genuine cases!"

I don't argue. It's true what he says. If you invite a bull to gore you, who can help? I spread the sheet I brought with me on the floor. The mosaic-patterned cement floor smells of Phenyl. It must be clean. The nurse gives us a blanket for Rama. Tulu plays with a plastic bottle putting a nail up its bottom. I want to shout at him for ruining a good bottle, but I can't. Suddenly I feel my eyes pricking. I busy myself straightening the edges of the sheet.

"We have to go now." Sanju Maa crouches beside me. "Amit is late for work. He's having a word with the doctor. They'll look after Rama. Here's some money for food and medicines." She looks over her shoulder as she presses the notes into my hand.

I join my hands in gratitude. For the money as well as Babu speaking for us. "I'll pay it back."

"Don't worry about that." Sanju Maa squeezes my shoulder.

Rama curls up on the sheet. His body is thin and wasted, his ribs sticking out. When he does go to work it's a miracle he manages to pull the trolley of rice gunnies. Not that I see any of the money. It all goes on the drink. But he doesn't beat me. The one time he went for me, I pulled out a piece of firewood from the cooking fire. It was a bluff. You can't raise your hand to your husband; you'll go to hell. But after that he never dared again, thank God.

I don't mind being poor or working hard. That is my fate. But isn't it also a husband's duty to provide for his wife like Amit Babu does? Why can't Rama be like him? I don't mean a bank manager. But Amit Babu is the breadwinner. He goes to the temple on all auspicious days and never touches a drop. He's respectable. He helps people like us. Why can't my husband be decent and god-fearing like that?

★

After two weeks in hospital, Rama is able to walk to the toilets without leaning on me. The doctor says he has to go to the de-addiction centre. He's been there before. The first time he ran away after three days. The second time he was very ill and scared. He stayed the duration. He was clean for four months. Then he went back to the bottle.

After dropping Rama at the centre, I reach home at dusk. The dark mouth of our single room opens to swallow us: my saris, Rama and Tulu's clothes draped over a clothesline; the thin mattress, the makeshift kitchen in the corner, the rice degchi upturned over my wok, spatula and ladle sticking out of the gap between the lip of the degchi and the rim – like the forked tongue of some monster.

This is the sum total of our universe. How scary things look when seen in a different light!

When I enter Sanju Maa's flat, brightness dazzles me: the sofa with the gilded wood frame and fixed upholstery where Amit Babu sits and watch the news; the coffee table with the curved legs; the magazines about big people. The dining table with the glass top and six chairs, also with fixed upholstery. Sanju Maa is bending over by the far wall beyond the dining table holding a cloth. I see the shards of something shattered, the spill and the dirty brown splashes on the wall. I love the colour of the wall paint, a shade like the core of the champa flower, like the golden-yellow of the light at sunrise. I cough. She starts and whips around, like someone was about to hit her.

"Oh, it's you!" She relaxes.

"The door was ajar, Maa."

"Why did you come? You should have rested after your long day."

"My head is full of garbage from sitting around for two weeks. Is Babu home? I wanted to thank him. The doctor was kind after Babu spoke to him."

"He's just gone out. An urgent meeting at the bank."

"Here Maa, give that to me. I'll clean it up."

"No, no. It's all right. I'll do it. I was rushing with a cup of tea for Amit and slipped."

Something stirs in my mind. Another time something had also broken. I think Ma had said a similar thing, but I can't recall. Tiredness fogs my brain.

"I'm sorry, Maa, you had a lot to do while I was away." I take the cloth from her hand. I didn't like that scared look on her calm face.

"Of course not. It's nothing to worry about." She pats me on the back and carefully cleans the wall with a sponge. It's plastic paint. Very expensive and for good reason. You can wipe off stains and no one would ever imagine it had been dirtied.

*

Rama comes home after a month. His yellowness has reduced. He eats most of his food and his bones don't stick out so much. He even reaches for me in the night, but can't get hard. I'm glad to turn over and go to sleep but feel a flicker of hope. He must be getting better. I ask him to rest but he goes to work after another month and gives me some money. I repay some of Sanju Maa's loan with it. If things carry on like this, I can start saving to buy a piece of land for my house.

I sleep and dream my house is being built. The masons putting brick on brick, the sounds of their trowels hitting the mixing pans as they pick up the mortar, then slap it in. I can feel the strength of the walls in my legs.

Then one evening as I walk home from work, I see a figure weaving about at the top of the lane. It takes me a moment to understand. Then I'm running and shouting. "What have you done, eh? Will you stop only when you're dead? Didn't you hear what the doctor said? You'll die if you drink again."

Rama is still clutching the empty plastic packet reeking of the fumes of his drink. I try to wrench it out of his hand. He pushes me away, staggering down the lane in his bare feet. I wish he would fall in a ditch or a truck knocks him down. That would be the end of my troubles.

"No! It can't be true," Sanju Maa says when I tell her. "I thought he'd given up for good this time."

"So did I," I laugh. "I dared to dream for a while. But dreams don't come true for people like us."

Rama comes home some nights. Other nights I don't know where he goes. When he stumbles in, he doesn't want the dal or vegetables I've cooked.

"Meat," he grunts. "Or salt dried shrimp."

"There's no money for those. Eat what I give you, or you can starve."

He glares and tries to rush at me, but falls over. I feed him making balls of the rice, squeezing a lime and adding some mustard oil to bring flavour to the food. The drink must have killed his taste. It's a fire that spares nothing. No wonder he asks for meat and sukhua.

"If you give up drinking, I will get you meat and fish every day." I shouldn't lie, but maybe I can tempt him to stop.

When he comes off his high in the morning, I try again. "Give up drinking. Look to God. He has saved your life so many times. We will be swept away if anything happens to you. Your son needs you. I need you. Look at Amit Babu. What a kind and caring husband he is. Can you learn nothing from him? We owe them so much. How will we repay them if you die?"

He staggers off scratching himself, this stick man with his pot belly which keeps getting bigger and bigger. As if he has a baby due any day.

One evening he collapses. I send Tulu to fetch Amit Babu and Sanju Maa. By the time Babu comes, the women of the neighbourhood have lit incense and the lamps of vigil.

"What's all this?" Amit Babu says. "Why the tears? Here! Maa has sent fish curry for you, Bhagya. She was insisting on coming, but I told her not to. She needs the smallest excuse to drop everything. Thank god I stopped her from taking a job. She can't even run our household, let alone work and home."

★

When Maa comes in the morning, Rama has been dead two hours. He's covered in a white sheet with a few marigolds placed on its edges. The neighbours are trying to find a Tempo to take him to the cremation ground. I'm not allowed to do anything, so I leave it to them. Maa drops to the floor, same as all the housemaids. She takes my hands. I can't stop my tongue.

"Everything is over for me. What is there to live for? I wished him ill. This is the punishment for my sin. I brought it on myself."

"No, no!" She wraps me in her arms. I cling to her. She doesn't break away. Instead, holding me tighter and sobbing, she cradles the back of my head, as if I were a child. It's me who pulls away in the end.

"They are preparing to take him away. I have to do a feast here and in our village."

"You can't afford that!"

"The neighbours say his soul will go to hell if I don't."

She looks like she's about to say something, but stops. I know she doesn't believe in these things. They are educated people, she and her husband, Amit Babu. But for us, it is everything. I hope she understands.

"Did you eat last night? Before…"

She knows how much I like her fish curry and always gives me some. She also knows it's a sin for widows to touch fish and meat. It raises the heat of the blood, brings impure thoughts.

"Yes, I did," I lie. "Tulu too. He licked his plate clean."

She sits by me, this upper-class woman, on the earthen floor of my one room hut. I hear the whisperings of the neighbour women and feel pride. But it is nothing compared to the sadness each time I look at the dead body by me and remember I am all alone in this world now. All alone to work and provide for myself and my child. I am ashamed, but I envy Sanju Maa her good fortune, her life, her husband.

"I will come with you to the cremation ground. And don't worry about the expense. You can have the feasts. No need to pay it back," she whispers.

I don't dare argue in case the neighbours hear and extend the list of dishes.

As the hired van trundles up, Amit Babu arrives.

"This is very sad, Bhagya. Very sad."

I press the corner of my sari-odhana into my eyes. "God's wish. What can we do against it? And Rama didn't help himself. Still, I'll pray for his soul. I'll offer a coconut at the temple."

"We'll help with a loan, of course," Babu says.

"Amit, I want to go with Bhagya to the cremation –"

His eyes flash. So fleeting, I wonder if I saw right.

"Have you forgotten the National Manager and his wife are arriving from Bombay? They were going to book a hotel. I invited them to stay with us. I'm picking them up from the airport in an hour. I only came to bring you the things for lunch."

"Couldn't you take them out? I'll be back in a few hours."

Amit Babu looks away and speaks in English. Quickly, biting out the words. I don't understand his words, but I wish I wasn't hearing them.

Babu strides away. Sanju Maa hangs her head a moment, then opens her handbag and presses money into my hand.

"Bhagya –"

"It's no problem, Maa, There wouldn't have been space in the van anyway. We are used to squeezing in but you can't travel like that."

I watch her walk to the car, her feet dragging like she has stones around her ankles. As she opens the door, she looks back at me. I have the strangest feeling then. As if all the while I had been dazzled, and only now I'm able to see.

My world has been turned upside down but Maa is sadder than me.

Gloria Hanley has lived and worked as a community midwife in Leeds for many years.

Her involvement in the Leeds community has been varied and extensive. She is the current chair of the Mary Seacole Nurses Association in Leeds and is working on erecting a bust in the Mary Seacole Gardens as a legacy to the first Black Jamaican nurse who served in the Crimean War. In 2019, Gloria published her first book *Everybody's Midwife*, a memoir of her work in multicultural Leeds. Over the years she has championed the health of the Black Community by arranging seminars and conferences on health and well-being, and was awarded a Certificate of Achievement by the Royal College of Nursing for outstanding contribution to the Black Community. Recently she has been awarded a certificate as a Windrush Pioneer who has paved the way for those who came after.

THE PARSONAGE

I alighted from the bus on a cold January morning after an hour's journey from my home in Moortown to Pudsey City Centre, ten miles away. The church bell on the steeple of the old stone-built Moravian church in Fulneck, Leeds, chimed as I walked towards the entrance.

I was a newly affiliated member of the church and was not familiar with the congregation. Today, a visiting preacher would be speaking; I was looking forward to his "message". At this church, the preachers delivered their message calmly. Before, I'd been attending a Pentecostal church for over 40 years where the preachers had been loud and fiery.

I opened the front door and entered the foyer that led to the main worship Sanctuary. Some of the regular congregation were already seated in their usual places at the back. I offered them a cheery good morning and headed for my seat in the third row of wooden benches, on the right-hand side of the church, next to an iron radiator.

A large crystal chandelier hung from the ceiling, lit up with about a dozen candle-shaped light-bulbs. There are four stained-glass windows at the front of the church, the central window depicting a white lamb carrying a flag with the words, *Our Lamb has conquered let us follow Him.*

I sat and bowed my head in quiet solitude when a gentle voice whispered, "Good morning". I looked up and was greeted by an English gentleman about sixty years old, wearing a grey suit with a grey shirt and a clerical collar. He had a welcoming smile on his slightly tanned face. This was, I supposed, the visiting minister. He had a familiar look about him, even though we had not met before.

"I am Reverend Gubi, and I am the visiting minister."

I stood up and shook his outheld hand before retaking my seat. The name was familiar. I learned that he was the grandson of the old Bishop in the Moravian church in St. Kitts, which I attended as a child.

I sat, closed my eyes, and took in the thunderous sound of the pipe organ playing "Amazing Grace".

A memory surfaced from my subconscious, taking me back to St. Kitts and this visiting preacher's grandfather. Bishop Gubi was a short old man with grey curly hair and a face full of folds and wrinkles. Having just retired, he was leaving the village church to return to England. He always smoked a wooden pipe unless he was preaching. The scent of tobacco hung over him like a cloud. He was well loved by his parishioners.

I was a teenager at the time.

My parents were devoted churchgoers and, barring illness, they attended church every Sunday with all their children in tow. We sat in the sixth row of wooden benches on the left side of the church. At 17, I became the youngest Board member, a Sunday School Kindergarten teacher, and a choir member.

It was announced one Sunday that a new minister would be arriving from Barbados to replace the bishop. The whole church was excited, especially when it was discovered that he was 27 years old, a Black man, and unmarried! All the ministers before had been white and married.

His first Sunday at the local church was as packed with people as a wedding ceremony. Young women turned up dressed in their finest, no doubt dreaming of becoming the minister's wife.

This idea must have been in my parents' heads, too. Their daughter – a minister's wife! One Sunday, they invited the young minister to Sunday lunch. The day before, my father caught the biggest chicken from the backyard, wrung its neck and had us girls pluck its feathers. We washed and seasoned it with the spices we cultivated in our back garden. We picked gungo peas from our garden and, with help of my brothers, shelled them. Then my mother prepared the rice.

After Sunday service, Mum hurried home to finish preparing the lunch. The Minister arrived at our home wearing his black ministerial suit and his dog collar. I noticed that the brilliantine hair grease seeped past his hairline down to his glistening forehead.

As he tucked into the meal of rice, peas, roast chicken, washed down with lemonade, I could feel his big brown eyes on my bosom, as if they were unbuttoning my blouse. The butterflies in my stomach began to play rounders. All the while my mother was encouraging me to "tell the minister how you are progressing with your piano lessons."

I felt sick and uncomfortable. I feigned a headache and excused myself from the table, leaving my parents chatting away with him. When I thought he had left, I returned to the dining area only to learn from my parents that he'd invited me to The Manse to discuss church business. My mum was giddy with excitement. In her head, she was probably buying her wedding dress as mother of the bride.

I pretended I was pleased but those warning butterflies had not abated.

When the day of the visit arrived, my mum dressed me in my best outfit – a turquoise knee-length dress with a high neckline, and black patent, high-heeled shoes. I had passed the ironing comb through my hair the night before and used twisted strips of brown paper to make curls. I used a burnt bit of cork to emphasize my eyebrows and smeared on red lipstick with some cotton wool.

I arrived at The Manse and gently tapped the door. My throat was constricted, and the butterflies in my stomach agitated. A plump old woman with a plaid head-kerchief and a pinafore over her floral cotton dress, opened the door. She grinned at me and invited me into the hall. She knocked on the drawing room door and opened it. The Minister was smiling when I entered. He had lovely white teeth.

He'd replaced his suit with a blue open-neck, short-sleeved cotton shirt and a pair of blue dungarees. I was thrown by his appearance. There they go again! The butterflies! He closed the door behind us and invited me to sit on a blue chaise lounge. He offered me what I guessed was a glass of the communion wine. I politely refused, asking for a glass of water instead. My throat felt parched.

We made stilted conversation until he invited me to the bedroom. My brain was in overdrive. I knew what was coming, but decided that I would go down fighting. He came to where I was standing near his wardrobe and drew me to him. My body stiffened when I felt his manhood prodding my front. He took a step back dropped his dungarees to the floor, and again he drew me close to him.

I opened my mouth to scream but he'd placed his hand over it. I tried to bite it without any success. We struggled for a short while and he agreed to remove his hand only if I promised not to scream.

I tried to open the door and realised he'd locked it.

"I want to go home," I said.

He opened the door and I rushed out of The Manse.

I found sanctuary on a bench under a large flamboyant tree which was near the main road in the village but out of sight of The Manse. I sat, pulse racing and heart throbbing, as I reflected on my escape from a situation that was suddenly out of my control.

I had heard many stories about enslaved women from our island's past being abused; of other women forced into similar situations by people they'd trusted.

As children, we were chastised with the belt by our parents, and any villager who thought that we were being disrespectful had the authority to cuff us around the ears. That had been all part of our upbringing. But not this! I am certain that sexual abuse occurred in the village but was swept under the bush fence. It was taboo even to mention it. Still, when I encountered it for the first time, my 18-year-old brain had turned to jelly.

I slowly walked home and headed for my bedroom. My parents were too preoccupied with my brother who was selected to play in the local school cricket match, to notice that I had returned home.

Shame and disgust filled my thoughts as I sat on my bed. I blamed myself for what I had just experienced. I knew that I could not tell my parents, not only because to speak of it was taboo, but who would believe an "impressionable" young woman?

There was also the possibility that Father would have paid the minister a visit with his machete.

I had always wanted to become a Minister of Religion or a Deaconess in the Moravian Church but something in me had drastically changed after that encounter. I was now the last person to arrive at Church and the first to leave when Sunday service ended. This meant that I had no further contact with the minister. I decided I needed to leave the village. I convinced my parents that I wanted to move overseas to train as a nurse with the promise that I would return after three years.

If my mother suspected that something had happened at The Manse to change my ambition so drastically, she never mentioned it. And I reflect, now, on how a single incident can so dramatically change a person's whole life trajectory.

Now 55 years later, I'm a retired nurse in England and I've still not returned to St. Kitts.

Nana-Essi J. Casely-Hayford, a scion of Griots and healers, effortlessly weaves her ancestral tapestry into a captivating narrative as a storyteller, writer, and a Creative Expression for Wellbeing Practitioner. Rooted in the tales spun by her grandmother, Nana-Essi writes from folkloric, mythical, and lived experiences. She has first-hand experience of storytelling's therapeutic, transformative powers. She's been inspired by dawn dialogues with her grandmother and the profound wisdom of elderly matriarchs. Nana-Essi embraces the profound values of the imagination.

THE ANTIDOTE

I re-watch the video message a friend has forwarded to me to make me aware of what he's been up to. Whitney Houston's "It's Not Right but It's Okay" is blaring out on the Magic Radio station. The song somehow gives me the strength to hold on to my dignity. How do I react when he comes home tonight?

I take a breath and try to concentrate on my shopping list!
a. Bitter Melon
b. Ashanti Plum
c. Guinea Hen Weed
d. Marigoule
e. Nkanfouo bariye (Nkanfouo Yam)
f. Abbobi kyekye

How could I not have known?

"Friends" I have lost touch with for over a decade are calling me, pretending to have my welfare at heart. More videos surface. Every new notification is a punishment. But I can't help looking. One of my new clients messages me, suggesting an appointment: meeting place, Emerald Dome Park. In two hours.

I leave home straight away. Emerald Dome Park is in breath-taking bloom, but is no salve for my shredded heart. How could I not have known? I trusted. No filters. Everything laid bare. How could I not have known?

The sun on my body feels like a deep tissue massage. I take in the wonderful fragrances of forget-me-nots, jasmine, and oriental lilies – scents I have been deprived of since the restrictions of lockdown. I can even smell the eucalyptus trees and lavender hedges nearby. Rows of rowan, wych elm, beech, ash, sycamore, horse chestnut, sweet chestnut and oak trees give the impression of crowds gathered for an illegal meet-up. Water features in the park become an orchestra in my head.

I think of what it means to be alive and how much I have taken for granted.

"How are you in boddi, child?"

An elderly woman appears in front me. There is a familiarity about her. The clinking of expensive Abyssinian bangles against the African ekra beads on both wrists remind me of the ladies of the Ceremonial Houses of Enstoolment back home in Ghana. I'm suddenly aching for my place of birth: the earthy aroma of new yam boiled in the early hours of the day to make eto eni kosua (eto fitaa – white mashed yam without palmoil) and eto kokor (mashed yam with spiced palm-oil and hard-boiled eggs). I think of the shots of akpeteshie gin lined up in miniature calabashes, offerings of alligator peppers and cola-nuts in the alcoves to the stool and medicine houses. She is, in spirit, an Anene – a white-necked African raven. I am certain of it. She would be one chosen for the council of elders – the shapeshifting clan that we are all aware of but never mention.

"I observe you admire nature and the beauty she gives to her creations, eh," she says.

"I'm well, thank you. And you?" I reply.

"My boddi keep me awake all hours ooo."

"I'm sorry to hear this. You and I can work with your GP to bring you to a reasonable level of pain management," I reply.

"GP sez I must not throw caution away. He sez I must take tentative steps to live in this new world the pandemic has created."

I am triggered. I'm about to move out of my body to hover above us. "Breathe, breathe, breathe," I tell myself. "Take deep, calming breaths. Keep alphabetising your shopping list —

g.   Crescentia Cujete Pulp
h.   Lemons
i.   Limes
j.   Tinctures: – Cayenne, Clove, Dogwood, Eyebright/Fairy Flax, Ginko Biloba/Maidenhair, Lion's Mane Mushrooms, Nascent Iodine, Olive Leaf, Valerian.

k. Prekese
(I must remember not to miss my 3:45pm consultation with Mother Djitaah. Something about Prekese always reminds me of her.)
l. Hwenstia

…that's it." I talk myself back into calmness and focus on my client.

"I need the list of medications you're on, also any allergies you might have to avoid any contraindications…"

"Kantra waat! Wat's dat?"

A few passersby turn to look at us.

"It's to check that the remedies I give you don't react badly against any medications you are already taking. It could be life threatening."

"Boddi tired and craving sunshine. Twenty months I live sequestered like nun in convent! It too much for me. You and GP I beg, make it so dat I get well to walk among people again ooo. I will go crazy if I lock up once more – yu hunderstand?"

I know how she feels. The thought of being indoors for another lockdown is terrifying.

"I do understand. We'll meet again in two weeks. I will have a conversation with your GP so I can give you the appropriate ointments and decoctions."

"Greet your Mamma for me eh," she waves and turns away.

I pull my mask down below my chin and take in again the glorious beauty of the park. I remember when it was a fly tip until the community came together to landscape it. He joined me to help with the landscaping. Even then I had my suspicions because of the venomous side-eyed glances I received from other women. I ignored my instincts and walked blindly into the relationship. I gave him the best years of my life.

Somehow my client manages to trip over her feet as she reaches one of the park exits. She falls heavily. I can see that by the way her body hits the ground. Several people run forward to help, including some park staff in their neon visibility vests. I run over too and offer to wait with her until an ambulance and paramedics arrives.

I watch my client, I imagine her petite figure teleporting to a medicine house in an African rainforest, surrounded by a council of elders and healers. In my mind, we are both swept up in a mist of light-coloured piebald feathers. Now she is the healer.

"Yu must calm your cardiac percussions ooo! Beating too rapid for your age."

She is right, the rhythm in my chest is such that I can barely breathe. The thin altitude air does not help either. I ought to be startled that an unconscious woman is communicating with me. However, the cloud of feathers swaddles us in a comforting quietness that settles me. Besides, I have spent a lifetime masking my abilities. They make no sense to people here in England.

"Child the feathers come together to carry us away."

Breathe, breathe...

m.   Akokomesa (Akan Basil)
n.   Replacement dadesen/cauldron
o...

My body ached to bear at least one child but... He rejected the idea. I respected his wishes and the topic was not brought up again. Yet, today, I find out about his three "baby mothers". Six children who are carbon copies of him. The world must not see me weeping.

We are now on the back of a prehistoric Omampam, scrambling over rocky terrain. I can hear the blood swishing through my veins. I can't catch my breath. My mind will not let go of the things I've just learned about my fiancé. And to think that everyone wanted to fashion their relationship on ours.

Breathe, breathe…

"Child, child, slow yu heart down; otherwise cardiac event and stroke go be yu boddi legacy," the elder reprimands.

The blood, roaring in my ears, makes me dizzy.
   p….
   Breathe, breathe…
   Now we are in the Medicine House where the elder is laid out on a treatment table. A woman mixes poultices and applies them to the abrasions on the elder's face.
   "She speak to you yet?"
   "No ma'am," I reply.
   "She was sent to you; do you know by whom?"
   "No ma'am."
   "You are consumed by your philandering partner." I look up startled, everyone but me knows about him!
   I sigh, bring myself back into the room and watch the treatment of the elder.
   The rest is a blur.
   Somehow, I make it to Aunty Iyabo's Cultural Food Store. My list is fulfilled. I sit calmly waiting for my fiancé to return. I have the YouTube videos set to play on his 98-inch Ultra HD Android P745K Smart TV – his absolute pride. I will wait till he is halfway through his meal of Nkanfouo bariye fufuo, eguse paste soup with goat meat, smoked catfish, fresh water blue crab and apofii, wild mushrooms and some okra, then I will press play.
   Of course, I have the antidote – tinned mimosa paste – to administer once the interrogation is done. I have no intention of being put away for premeditated murder or manslaughter. Absolutely not! He is in for the biggest chastisement of his life and he will not forget it in a hurry.

He arrives with a large bouquet of flowers. A mix of vibrant, orange-coloured oriental lilies, multi-coloured bird of paradise plants, anthurium, fern and bougainvillea. He sniffs the air as he hands them over to me and pecks me on the cheek.

"Wait, don't tell me," he says, his right hand raised. "You have my favourite laid out on the table for me. Eguse soup. Mmm, mmm, mmm! What's the occasion?"

He walks into the downstairs washroom, chatting away as he washes and dries his hands. Taking a seat at the dining table, he asks about my day, starts ladling soup onto the fufu and tucks in as though he hasn't eaten for days. I watch and wait patiently, head tilted to the right. Then I press play on the TV, walk up to the table and place the vase of beautiful flowers beside him. The bouquet comes to life and starts twining up his arms and torso. His terror is satisfaction enough. I sit back and enjoy, while Nancy Wilson's "Guess Who I Saw Today" plays in the background.

Saluka Saul is a writer of Guyanese origin based in the North of England. She has published academically, specialising in Ancient Black History. Her present writing life has been energized by her past experiences, including being a critical reviewer for *TOUCH* and *Black Filmmaker* magazines in the 1990s. Following her graduation in Social Anthropology and History of Photography, she was a photographer for the Phoenix Dance Company. She has recently completed a Post Graduate degree in Writing for Performance & Digital Media at the University of Leeds. She's been linguistically intoxicated by the works of James Baldwin, Maya Angelou and Dave Chappelle. Saluka produces writing that has an underlying social message.

BEST ROOM MISADVENTURES

I

A common feature of many traditional Caribbean 1970s UK households was the "Best Room". It was only used for guests. Children were never allowed to enter it. This left them wondering, what on earth did the elders get up to behind the door?

As a child, I dreamt of having a best room when I grew up. Today, my own Victorian house has a "Best Room" downstairs: twenty-square feet with twelve feet high walls. I reserve it for special dinners, birthdays, parties with giant sound systems or just general storage. Such a variety of things have taken place inside that room, I can no longer call it my "Best Room".

Take for instance the year our father passed away around Mischievous Night. Before we laid him to rest, we held an "open coffin" where, for two days, his friends turned up and wished him a good passage. One was his best friend, Clifton, who lived next door – a refined, elderly Caribbean gentleman who knew all of Dad's children since we were babies. Another "friend" was our mother, who he hadn't seen since their divorce in the late 1980s. How lovely that she got to share a glass, or ten, of brandy with him before his physical departure. I'm confident that Dad really appreciated that.

It was better than him lying alone, cold, isolated and unloved in a funeral parlour in the all-white village where he lived. In fact, the last time we visited him, I was called the "N" word by an extremely elderly Caucasian woman as I was getting off the single-decker village bus. I really wanted to tear off her pound-shop wig and force feed her sticky toffee tissues down her crinkled chin-neck.

Dad had lived in this village for two decades now, having moved in with his white girlfriend from the 1980s, who became a rather troublesome wife at the very end. They had two amazing children, a boy and a girl. He was a very good father. All five of his children adored him and each other. There was no such thing as half-siblings in our family.

It was not until three days after he died that we were told he'd passed away. It was imperative that Martha and I brought his body home for his final passage – a repatriation of sorts. Our house was where he loved to stay in his pyjamas all day – without judgment. It was where he consumed copious amounts of home-cooked chicken soup. Here, our father had lived twelve times longer than predicted by the oncologists.

We travelled to a cold Withusborough in Yorkshire to retrieve his body. Withusborough – one of those picturesque towns on the outskirts of cities, endowed with greenery and still harbouring racial prejudice. Back home, we placed him in the Best Room.

It so happened that it was Mischievous Night, which we detested – along with Halloween, Bonfire Night and Christmas. They are grim reminders of broken families for some, and celebration for others. To us, they were annoying, unavoidable parts of our calendar.

Me and my twin sister, Martha, used to just "dance it out" with loud reggae music, heavy bass lines and insane dance moves. Good job that nobody else was watching.

On this particular Mischievous Night, we could not dance it out otherwise people would know we were at home and we did not want any trick or treaters knocking on our door to disturb our deceased dad in the Best Room.

My twin, Marvellous Martha, disappeared upstairs. I stood for a while with my back against the hefty wooden front door, pondering my next move.

There was a knock at our door. I suddenly remembered we'd ordered jerk chicken a few hours before. Or perhaps this was our first trick-or-treat children knocking. I resentfully opened the door and was greeted by the incredible odours of jerk spice. A tall, slender Jamaican man named Miguel stood outside holding an aluminium wrapped parcel of edible ecstasy. Mischievous Martha was good friends with Miguel and everyone in the local community knew that he could chef the hell out of any Caribbean dish.

Miguel looked past me up at the staircase and burst out laughing, shaking his long locs in disbelief. I turned around to view my twin sister descending the stairs in a homemade Halloween outfit put together in less than three minutes: shredded fishnet tights and one stiletto shoe with a heel barely attached to it; a ripped red dress underneath an oversized black faux-fur coat. Her face was smothered in make-up, as if she had applied it to her eyes and lips with a spatula. My sister waited until Miguel finished laughing.

"Fancy a treat...?" she asked, throwing him a grin.

"What is it?" Miguel shrugged, wary now because he knew Martha loved to play tricks. "Come," she smiled. Tottering on her single high heel, she led him to the Best Room.

"Where is the treat then?" Miguel asked.

It was then he saw the open coffin with our father laid out in it, his eyes open just a slit as if observing his twin daughters having their fun. Miguel turned and rushed towards the front door. Me and Martha could barely control our laughter.

For a great part of the night, trick-or-treaters turned up, knocked the door and we enticed them into the Best Room. Without exception, they screamed and promptly ran out.

Close to morning, we grew tired of the game. Martha and I entered the Best Room, each with a tall glass of brandy and a single ice cube, no mixer – just the way Dad liked it. We sat next to him; thought we detected a side smile on his deeply bronzed and wrinkled face. We talked to him for hours, remembering all the good times with him. Like when we did our weekly shopping and he went around the aisles "tasting" grapes and other foods that we might or might not buy. Or the excitement of childhood Saturdays when he baked mounds of fresh bread, picked sweetcorn cobs from the greenhouse; or cooked a delicious chicken feast for the whole family. Without fail, Dad always cooked on Saturdays after washing his yellowy-orange Datsun car.

The next morning, the undertakers came to pick him up. We watched the four smartly dressed men struggle to close the lid. It was as if the old man hadn't finished with the fun. Eventually, they managed to lift him off the chrome trolley and take him out of the Best Room. At the door, there was the curved corner wall to negotiate. And, as if in one last act of rebellion, the men at the back lost their grip of the coffin. We watched it drop to one side in seriously slow motion. Once again, the laughter was uncontrollable.

Typical of Dad we thought, stubborn even in death.

Honestly, there has never been a single knock on Mischievous Night since that day.

II

Sub-woofer blasting beautiful bass, my sister, Martha, and I are dancing like no one is watching, our hair gelled back like Latino convicts. Being Guyanese we can pass for many different races when we feel like it. We are getting hyper in the Best Room, preparing to shoot off to Manchester to see some of America's finest gangster rap artists, live in concert. Before we left, we prayed in the Best Room for the chance to meet the artists after the show. We had successfully done so many times.

As usual, we arrive late at our hotel, having never driven to this side of Manchester before. Our hotel was not easy to find. These city roads seemed to have their own set of side roads that took us all over the place.

We arrive at the city-centre's basic hotel room, drop our overnight bags on the floor and rush to spruce ourselves up in our cubby hole bathroom. We both down a stupid amount of brandy and step out in denim hot pants, cigarettes tucked into the right back pocket, mobile phone in the left. We are wearing warm jumpers and knee-high camel coloured Ugg boots. My signature diamond socks are sticking out of the top of my boots. Martha and I are looking forward to a heavy duty rave.

The student venue is already packed when we arrive. The place is full of harmless wannabe gangsters dressed in student jeans, hippy logo t-shirts and sheepskin coats. Most of them look like they are studying philosophy, with a music module chucked in. Even the Black ones.

The Seedy Moss Crew are already running up and down the stage with mics in hand, rapping about North American stuff. We find ourselves at the back of the venue, miles away from the stage. We gently elbow our way to the very lip of the stage. We are just about to make it when a terrifically tall teenager decides to push me. What to do...? I hate conflict but I am a believer in survival of the fittest and we have a specific goal. I push Tall Boy back and press my whole body to the stage front.

A mammoth of a man is on stage staring down at us. His expression never changes once. He reminds me of Tommy Lister Jnr. "Big Deebo" is his name for the rest of the evening. My twin, Martha, flirts with Big Deebo for the next hour while she dances to the brassy beats and N-words on repeat.

When the concert is over and the crowd disperses, we remain where we are to avoid getting crushed. Big Deebo comes towards us, points and shouts, "You! You! Backstage!" I turn to Tall Teenager, wink and quickly clamber on to the stage towards gangster rap heaven.

We make our way backstage and try not to look down on the four outraged teens who probably had school the next day. The main rapper, Zed Teez, looks angry for some reason. He's shut the door on everyone. He's lost my respect to this day. Those four young girls had gone to great lengths to sneak out on a school night, dressed up like women in their early twenties, and somehow managed to get backstage. Two minutes of his time would have made their effort worthwhile.

I decide to forget this. Martha and I walk back to the hotel. Turns out the show was not that far from the hotel. Martha shows me a scrap of paper with Big Deebo's phone number on it. She does not waste time that girl! What a night! We down the remaining brandy, tucking ourselves up into a duvet.

Martha's phone rings.

"You are joking me!" I say.

It is Big Deebo inviting us to their hotel. It is three in the morning, we are battered, not too sure where we are and, more importantly, too high to drive. We have no money for a cab, no cash at all. But! We're about to get acquainted with some real-life hard men. Never bothered us before.

What do you do with one of those once-in-a-lifetime moments? You put on your Ugg boots over your pyjamas, drive round and round on left/right, right/left ten-lane roads covering the same path several times; getting dangerously lost, looking for some plush hotel that suddenly appears in a spooky industrial site.

A string of shiny black Jeeps are cruising through the car park with sweet thick-smelling smoke seeping through the window. Zed Teez is still moody, so we chill with Big Deebo who scrunches his gigantic frame into the back of my Mini, bent over in an upside-down L shape. I try not to turn around too often. The rest of the Seedy Moss Crew park their Jeeps and go into the hotel.

A super slender guy appears in the car park. Through the fog in front of my windscreen, I watch him take away one of the parked Jeeps. I turn around to my sister and the upside-down L-shaped Deebo, both deep in gangster rap convo.

"What the hell that's all about?" I ask.

"Oh yeahhhh… they said they gon take them Jeeps away for the weed smoking. Somebody must have snitched on my Crew. Can't believe it's still illegal in Great Britain. Shiiiiiit."

I'll get that Jeep back soon."

He exits my car and leaves on foot. Martha and I stare at each other. After what feel like twenty minutes, Big Deebo drives back into the car park, parking the shiny black Jeep right where it was, initially. Again, Martha and I stare at each other.

We decide to go back to our city-centre hotel. I leave my car and jump in Big Deebo's giant vehicle. In the driver's seat of a four-by-four, he no longer looks like a ludicrously large L-shaped, prison-ready security guard.

We get to the hotel and Martha invites the big man inside. I sit on the double bed, baffled as to how they obtained chunks of weed in England when they arrived from the U.S. just a few hours ago.

As if he's been reading my mind he says, "Oh yeahhhh… brought that weed through customs easy, shiiiiiit."

Sitting upright on the tiny chair in our hotel room, he offers me a spliff. I decline and leave Martha sitting on Big Deebo's giant lap, chatting away; wondering for a split second if this beast of a man might kill me in my sleep. I eventually dropped off.

Big Deebo and Martha speak nearly every day for the next seven days. The next time we hear from the Seedy Moss Crew was a couple of weeks later when we receive a phone call from Paris Charles-de-Gaulle airport, Immigration office. I thought it was some kind of wind-up as I did not hand out our home phone number.

It was not a wind-up. Martha had given Big Deebo the home phone number. The French immigration officer wanted to confirm that these detained artists were staying at my house, before allowing them to come out of the Parisian airport and make their way to London.

Staying at MY house! That is not happening, I decide.

And it didn't.

Savitri Pema qualified as an Educational Psychologist (Ch. Psychol.) with an M.Ed from the University of Leeds, and M.Sc. (Psychol.) from Sheffield University. She has worked extensively in the fields of special educational needs, mental health, and race and equality training in the UK and abroad.

She started her creative writing journey by sharing stories with her family of her early life in India, and the impact of displacement and adjustment in British society. She has a particular interest in how identity is formed and reformed. She has published a book of short stories based on her experiences. She has been published in Psychological Services to Schools: *Threads of Life* (Heathcliffe Press); several poems in *Unbroken Bonds: Connected Through Corona*; in *Mui Magazine* published by the L.S.E; in the anthology *Weighted Words* by the Peepal Tree Press's Readers and Writers Group. She has several poems in *The Poem is Part of the Eye* (2023) and short stories in *The Story Sown Far* in the Bite Sized Books series 2023.

PEBBLE ON A BEACH

*"What you are is what you have been.
What you'll be is what you do NOW."*
— The Buddha.

I don't know for how long we sat staring at the red-brick bungalow. It could have been a few seconds, or hours. It was as if time had stopped within the warm bubble of the car, our linked hands creating our own private world. It started again, along with my heartbeats, as Geoff gently loosened his fingers from mine to reach into the back for the bunch of mixed roses we had bought.

"Shall we?" he asked, coming around to open my door. Watching as I tidied my hair for one last time, he whispered, "You look lovely. Don't worry."

He handed me the flowers as I got out of the car. "Here, you'd best give her these. It was your idea. I never bring her flowers, so she'd be suspicious."

A gust of wind whipped my freshly shampooed hair across my face. As I swept it off, I caught a movement in the window and thought I saw the lace curtains flutter.

"You okay, sweetheart?" he asked, tucking stray strands of hair behind my ears, his fingers lingering on my cheek. I shivered as the warmth from his hand left my skin, despite the thick woollen coat I was wearing.

I nodded, still thinking of the eyes behind the curtains. I wanted to tell Geoff that I needed to return to the safety of the car, away from the flood of memories that threatened to drown me. Instead, I forced a smile, because I knew how much it meant to him. I'd put off this visit so many times before, I was afraid it would never happen if I turned back now.

"You're sure?" he asked, his finger hovering on the doorbell.

I hesitated. Now I was suddenly eighteen again, standing on a different doorstep, staring up into Geoff's father's frowning face, his bushy brows meeting over a bulbous nose.

His glittering hazel eyes had flickered over my face and down to my bare brown legs before resting on his son. Surely, Geoff had told his father about me?

The door's sudden opening brought me back to the moment.

"Come in…" she shouted over the sound of the chimes, her lined face crinkling up into a smile, making her eyes disappear into the folds of her eyelids.

There was a faint smell from a bunch of pink, red and white roses on a table in the hallway. The roses sat in a sparkling crystal vase beside a clock that ticked loudly.

"Come on in and get warmed up out of that bitter wind," she said, ushering us into the lounge.

"I'll get a vase for these, Mam." Geoff pointed to the roses in my hand. "Do you still keep them at the back of the cupboard by the back door?" He gave her a quick peck on the cheek.

I knew what he was doing. He wanted me to be alone, to give her a chance to talk, but I wished he hadn't disappeared like that.

A quarter of a century of hurt rippled through my body as I faced his mother. She ran a hand over her white poodle curls, which framed her face neatly. When I'd first met her, all those years ago, they fell from her head in bouncy auburn waves.

I retreated inwardly from her gaze. What did she see? The same unwelcome teenager or the woman I now was?

She moved towards me, her hand held out "I… I always thought you and our Geoff were… It was a dreadful mistake that shouldn't have…"

"These are for you." I thrust the roses at her with a trembling hand.

As I looked at the veined outstretched hand, a face floated into my mind. Geoff's father had stayed in the doorway for a long time, staring without saying a word. A burning sensation in my stomach had risen to my throat which became hiccups that rattled through my body.

"A glass of water for our Geoff's… friend, please, Brenda," his father had called into the house as he turned to go back inside.

Geoff had followed his father inside. We had carried on to the back of the house into a small kitchen where a tall slim woman was juggling steaming pots on a stove. The windows had misted up, despite the back door being open over a cobbled back alley.

"Sit down, lass, and take little sips, otherwise you'll choke," she'd said, holding out a glass of water to me.

I had done as she'd instructed, looking up at Geoff, a thousand questions in my head.

He answered the one I hadn't asked. "Mam's a nurse."

But before he could say any more, an older version of Geoff had popped his head around the door, dressed in smart trousers, white shirt and grey tie. I assumed that this was Geoff's older brother. He was followed by a young girl of about twelve.

"This is Karen, my little sister." Geoff had put an arm around the girl, giving her a quick hug.

"Not so little," she'd retorted, going up on tiptoe beside him.

Although she was nearly my height, at just over five feet, she was not yet as tall as the rest of the family, who were all at least six feet.

"And I'm Dave, the clever handsome one," his brother said, coming to where I was sitting.

"You mean the boring one, don't you?" Geoff had rallied. "You can tell the way he's dressed that he sits at a desk crunching numbers all day."

Dave had pointed at Geoff's trousers. "Did you know those bell bottoms used to be curtains, and the shirt, one of me sister's dresses? And look at his long hair! It's obvious he can't afford to go to a barber on his student grant," he'd said, smoothing down his own neat, short hair.

Grateful for the friendliness, I'd laughed in the middle of a hiccup, spraying water all over the floor. "Oh… oh… I'm so so sorry," I'd spluttered, looking around for something to mop it up with.

"It's only water, hinny. Don't worry." Geoff's mother was already on her knees with a cloth. "Now away with ya. Get out of my kitchen into the dining room where tea's laid on. I'll bring in the scones when they're ready. Go on!"

Piles of sandwiches and cakes were set on plates with patterned doilies. At one end of the table stood a very tall brown teapot, as if guarding the food. I sat between the two brothers, who continued to banter, making me giggle as they recounted the antics they used to get up to.

Things were more subdued after their father joined us: polite if distant, concentrating on eating his meal. Linda, Geoff's married sister had come in to join us for a cup of tea. She didn't say much to me, but kept looking at my hair, at one point running a hand over the long black waves. I was a bit embarrassed at first, but she smiled so sweetly at me, so I decided she was just being nice.

"Now you've met everyone except for our Alison and her husband, Paul, Sita. Maybe you and Geoff can go round to theirs tomorrow?" Geoff's mother said.

Looking around the table at Geoff's family, I had yearned for mine. It had fractured when I was fifteen. My parents had to go back to India to look after my paralysed grandmother, leaving us with my older brother and sister-in-law. It would be nice to be part of a big family like this.

I took another bite of the delicious scone, slathered with homemade jam and thick cream, and leant back in my chair, chiding myself for being over-sensitive about Geoff's father's apparent detachment.

That night we had crawled back to the house exhausted

from dancing at a nightclub with Dave and his girlfriend. Geoff and I hadn't talked much about how we felt about each other, but I knew he liked me a lot, and I'd felt really close to him. I decided that I was being paranoid.

Next morning, I'd waited in my room until I thought everyone had finished in the bathroom. I came down to find Geoff's sister, Karen, feeding their dog in the kitchen.

"This is Sooty. I'm going to take her for a walk," she'd said, unhooking a lead from a coat rack. "Do you like dogs? You can come with me if you like. I usually let her have a run before breakfast."

"That's kind of you. I could do with some fresh air. I was really hot in the night with the thick bedcovers," I told her, pulling on my coat.

"My granny sleeps in the room you're in, and she piles on the blankets, even in summer."

"Is she your nani or dadi?" I asked as we crossed the road to a green area where Karen let the dog off the lead to run ahead.

"Huh? She's me gran."

"Sorry. I mean is she your father's mother or mother's mother? You see, in our culture we have a term for every relationship which lets you know exactly how you are related to a person."

"Oh that's cool. She's me mam's mother."

"Then she's your Nanima. Will she be back before we go back to Newcastle tonight? I'd like to meet her."

"You won't be able to, 'cause Mam sent her to my uncle's house for the weekend."

"Oh no, I feel terrible now. I could have slept on the floor. That's what my friend Maria and I do anyway, in her flat. We take it in turns, then hide the bedding in case the landlord comes in."

"Why do you do that? Don't you have a bed of your own?" Karen turned a puzzled face towards me.

I wondered how much Geoff had told his family about me. It wouldn't be easy to explain to a nine-year-old with no knowledge of other cultures why I'd ended up hiding in my friend's flat. Instead, I asked, "Maybe Geoff and I could go to meet your Nanima at your uncle's house, if it's not too far?" Karen took a ragged breath before blurting out, "I heard Mam and me Dad saying they'd better get her away just in case."

"In case?"

Karen didn't answer. She walked ahead, scuffing her toes in the grass. I felt sorry for her, being caught up in adults' secrets, poor girl. I caught up with her and put a hand on her arm.

"It's all right Karen. It was because of me, wasn't it?"

"I don't know… but she's old, you know, and might say something," Karen muttered.

After that we watched the antics of the dog as it scampered around sniffing at things that only he could smell. The secret world of a dog seemed a magical place to me, one that I wished I could escape to.

We went in through the back door so that we wouldn't dirty the carpet in the hallway, which was probably why they didn't hear us come in. A gruff male voice, louder and more strident than the others, carried into the kitchen.

"Of all the pebbles on the beach, why did you pick this un! You never had any sense, our Geoffrey, and going to a fancy university in Newcastle has addled yer brain."

A long pause, then the mother's voice disagreeing and placating at the same time.

"You keep out of it, Brenda. Working with darkie nurses is one thing, marrying one is another."

Karen had looked at me to see if I'd heard, and my face must have given her the answer because she went red, avoiding my gaze.

"That's what me Dad's like, but he don't mean any harm you know," she'd whispered.

My heart was pounding so hard I thought it might jump out of my rib cage. Through the crack in the door I heard

Geoff's father's voice. "Marriage is tough enough, lad, without bringing half-castes into the world."

Then the door had swung open to reveal the tableaux inside. The three men, with the same thick hair and big bulbous noses were seated around the table, untouched teacups in front of them. Geoff's mother was sitting with the brown pottery teapot in front of her, twisting a lacy handkerchief around her fingers.

For a moment no-one spoke.

"We've just come back from taking Sooty for her morning walk across the beck." Karen's shrill voice sliced through the silence.

The father spoke as if there was nothing untoward. "Good girl, Karen. Mind you clean her paws and rub her down before she comes into here." He picked up his teacup to take a sip.

I looked at Geoff. His hazel-flecked eyes were shuttered, his left leg striking the table leg with the tip of his blue suede shoe.

"I've found the vase, Mam." Geoff's voice brought me back from my reverie. He walked into the lounge holding a pretty crystal vase. "It'll need a wash first," he added.

"You shouldn't have bothered, but it's very kind of you. You can never have too many flowers. Especially roses," she said, taking the flowers into the kitchen. "You two sit down and I'll mash tea."

That's when I noticed the table crammed with sandwiches, salad, and yes, scones with jars of homemade jam and cream.

Geoff draped an arm over my shoulder and planted a kiss on top of my head. "Told you it'd be okay, didn't I?"

"I don't know, Geoff. It's brought it all back, all the –"

"There we are. Freshly mashed," his mother said, bustling in with a smaller replica of the brown teapot.

Here we were again twenty-five years later – after both our recently failed marriages.

In the end, I was the one who had decided to have an

arranged marriage with a man from my own religion and culture, when the strain of what had happened between Geoff's father and I, made me question a future with Geoff.

As soon as I had stepped into his mother's lounge, the first thing I'd noticed was a framed photograph on the mantelpiece. Geoff's father.

Now, I walked over to look at it more closely whilst Geoff was in the kitchen helping his mother. I smiled as I listened to their laughter coming from the kitchen.

I picked up the photograph and, gazing into the same hazel flecked eyes as his son's, asked "What would you say to us today?"

Shani Alexander was born in Carriacou, Grenada, where she spent the first 12 years of her life, before moving to Huddersfield, West Yorkshire.

She has an undergraduate degree in journalism and a master's degree in international relations. She has been working as a journalist for more than 12 years, and has written about the energy sector, employment law and healthcare.

She spent four years living in Singapore. While there, she travelled around Asia and Australia, learned martial arts and experienced different cultures. She took some time away from work and moved to France for a year to learn French. She now resides in the UK and enjoys reading books of all genres, while writing and learning French.

AT THE FUNERAL

We were all gathered again at St Thomas's church, on Manchester road, in Huddersfield, to say goodbye to one of our own. I didn't know him but he was from Carriacou and therefore one of ours. Besides my mum knew him.

It was a crisp, cold January day. The sky was clear.

When we arrived, people were milling around outside the church, greeting old friends and acquaintances. The body was yet to arrive. My mum introduced me to those who'd seen me recently at my step-dad's funeral.

"We all have to go sometime," someone said, as they greeted my mum.

We stood outside. Talking. Watching. Waiting. People turned up wearing winter coats of varying colours and designs. I didn't have appropriate shoes. My feet were cold. I was wearing tights but my strappy heels offered little protection from the weather. After a while, my feet couldn't handle it anymore. I left my mum and went into the church.

It was almost full. I took a seat at the front, facing the congregation. I put my bag on a seat next to me, reserving it for my mother. I looked around at a myriad of different shades of brown faces, some solemn, some smiling, some deep in thought. They were Kayaks and Grenadians and, I guessed, the odd Jamaican. All gathered to say goodbye to one of our own.

The women behind me were voicing their observations out loud. "Ay, ay, whey she tink she going? She forget this is a funeral? Her dress, short, short, and she ain't even wearin tights in this cold."

I smiled.

We stood up as they came in with the coffin. My mum walked in with her friend and they sat together.

As the service began, it hit me again: me, all by myself. No one next to me. No one to talk to or even whisper something to. Everyone else appeared to be with a partner, a friend, a family member. I closed my eyes trying to hold back the rush of tears. My chest wanted to burst open. My mind wandered to all the places, and all the times I've been alone: on a plane, a train; in Japan, Thailand; at a restaurant, the cinema... and now in a church at a funeral. I thought I'd gotten used to it.

I stared at the coffin in front of me. We die alone but does that mean that we must live alone?

My attention was brought back to the present as everyone stood up to sing a hymn.

I watched the sunrise lighting the sky,
Casting its shadows near.
And on this morning bright though it be,
I feel those shadows near me.

And then I broke. I had to put a hand over my mouth to stop the sobs from bursting out of me. My legs were shaking. I stopped singing – the same song they sang at my stepdad's funeral, less than a year before. I just stood there clothed in my loneliness, letting the grief wash over me.

I'd been to other funerals since my stepdad's, and sung the same song, but the loneliness I felt now, combined with the grief, threw me into a turmoil. I wanted to disintegrate under the weight of my emotions but I took a couple of deep breaths and pulled myself together.

I watched some members of the family of the man who died crying silently. A woman sat down, head bowed as she, too, was overcome with grief. I knew she'd lost her sister a couple of months before.

I hugged myself, bowed and waited for the hymn to end. Then we all sat down. I took a tissue, dried my eyes and blew my nose. There were prayers, readings, and more hymns.

When the service ended and the coffin was carried out, I slowly walked out with the rest of the mourners. I found my mum waiting for me outside. I followed her to the cemetery.

In the time it took for me to walk from the car to the graveside, my feet felt like lead. They barely held me up. My mum said we didn't have to be at there, we could go to the reception. But I wanted to be there.

As they lowered the coffin in the ground, loved ones threw rum, cigarettes, flowers, and a handful of dust into the grave. Then the men grabbed their shovels. Some had exchanged their church shoes for wellington boots.

Someone began to beat a drum, a banjo joined in, and we started singing hymns again.

Some people sang in tune, some were tone deaf. There were small groups in conversation. Others were being introduced to friends or saying hello to a relative they hadn't seen in a long time. Many were laying flowers on the graves and tombstones of their loved ones.

Then a bottle of brandy was passed around to warm ourselves against the cold; to offer a libation for those who'd passed.

My mum had her arms around me on one side. Someone else came and put their arm around me on the other. We stood there drinking, singing, watching, waiting, sympathising, and even laughing at times. I forgot my feet. I forgot my loneliness. I forgot my grief.

It took about an hour for the men, taking turns, to cover the grave. And then it was over. Back in the car, with the heating on full blast, I began to feel like I had regained my feet.

The hall was warm. The tables were covered with white cloths and set out with juices, wines, and sweets. The chairs were covered in white with ribbons tied behind the back, like bows. And there was music.

I sat with my mum who filled me in on the latest gossip – some woman who had left her husband for a younger man. Others joined us at the table and other conversations started.

Faces I'd not seen in a while popped by to say hello. Others I'd known all my life were there. I was introduced to those I'd never seen before. We chatted.

They asked where I was from. I said Carriacou. Who is your family, they asked. I told them. They knew my grandmother.

We ate. We drank. We talked. We laughed. I asked a quiet woman how she knew the family. She didn't, she said, she came for the food. Later I saw her walking into the kitchen with a container.

We drank some more and then we danced.

And suddenly I saw this death and these people gathered here for what they were – celebrants of a life just passed.

Perhaps this is the only certainty. In death, everyone goes alone but while we are alive, what really matters is the thing that brought us here together – community and belonging.

Jason Allen-Paisant is a Jamaican poet and writer whose work examines the ways in which Afro-diasporic artists and communities shape their lives through embodied, living philosophies. He's a graduate of the University of the West Indies (Mona) and of the University of Oxford, where he earned a DPhil in Medieval and Modern Languages, with a dissertation on theatre from the English- and French-speaking Caribbean. He is currently a professor of Critical Theory and Creative Writing at the University of Manchester. Jason is the author of two critically acclaimed poetry collections. The first, *Thinking with Trees*, won the 2022 OCM Bocas Prize for Poetry. The second, *Self-Portrait as Othello*, is a Poetry Book Society Choice and the winner of the 2023 Forward Prize for Best Collection; and the 2023 T.S. Eliot Prize. He is the author of *Théâtre dialectique postcolonial*, and a philosophical monograph, *Engagements with Aimé Césaire: Thinking with Spirits*, is published with Oxford University Press. His memoir, *The Possibility of Tenderness*, will be out with Hutchinson Heinemann in 2025. Jason lives in Leeds, England, with his wife and two children.

A DIFFERENT KIND OF PLAY

Tonight he found himself on the metro with Laurent, Agnès, Clara, and Mathilde. Mathilde, whom he'd met back in Oxford, was studying at the École Normale Supérieure. Laurent was her long-time boyfriend; Clara and Agnès were friends she'd known since primary school. Marcus can't remember how the conversation started, but the group began to talk about their first memories from the age of three, four, even two. They are laughing. In a moment like this, laughing is what you do to show that you're a friend. It's cute. A safeguard against ugliness. At the École normale, you chuckle, titter, and cackle about things that are cute, "interesting". When you're not debating, showing off your intellectual prowess, you're laughing at something cute. Nothing gets messy.

But tonight, Marcus couldn't help himself from getting messy. Perhaps he wanted to test out his capacity to be messy, to feel how the truth sounded on his tongue – the story of his life that he'd guarded from these people, with their cute childhoods, and their interesting lives: their trips to museums, their holidays at the Club Med, their suave nuclear families. Whatever it was, he decided to flirt with his first memory. This was funny, he thought; surely they'd find it funny.

It came back to him rather vividly. The first memory Marcus had was of destroying a toy helicopter, one his old cousin, Sister Vads, had sent him from America. Sister Vads was a relative by his grandfather's side and had lived in New York from before he was born, but for whatever reason, Sister Vads used to send stuff for him – ganzies, shoes, onesies – when he was a baby, and, for the first and only time, a toy helicopter. Mama, his grandmother, had nobody else overseas who'd send stuff for little Marcus.

Mama would hide the helicopter from Marcus and take it out occasionally for him to play with. It was pure joy whenever this happened. It had a remote control that would allow it to levitate, up, up to the ceiling, its propeller whirring. Marcus was enthralled by this. Such toys were rare in the district where he lived. He wasn't aware of any other child in Coffee Grove who'd had a battery-controlled toy. They all played with things they made themselves, out of avocado seeds, wood, abandoned juice boxes... But Marcus had his levitating helicopter from America. Nothing would give him more joy than to show it off to his friends. He wanted to take it with him down to his neighbour, Mother Scille, where her grandchildren and many other kids came to play. But Mama would only give him the helicopter for ten minutes or thereabouts – a nonsensically short time.

He had no idea where Mama kept it. The toy would appear in her hands as if by magic. Was she hiding it under the bed, in a grip, under some piece of plastic, up behind the Celotex of the ceiling? Or perhaps in the barrel with the other rare gifts she had received from foreign. She would make a silly chortling giggle and say, "Come Marcus! Copter! Copter time... See copter here." And, overwhelmed, he would rush towards the copter. Then after a short while, Mama would come to take it away. Marcus would be forced to stay outside while she went to hide it, and the copter would remain hidden for days – an eternity, really. "I don't want you to mash it up. That's enough for today. Tomorrow you get it again."

But he did not want to play with the helicopter tomorrow; he wanted it now. Why shouldn't he have it now? Why did he always have to wait, to not have too much? What was too much playing? And this denial that extended over everything, this endless no? He didn't think the other parents would've frustrated their children like this. Save it till tomorrow!... Why did Mama want so much to prevent him from being happy?

One day when she'd brought out the toy and gone back into the house, the boy, who was three plus, picked up a rock from the front yard and began battering the helicopter. Blinded by rage, he slammed the rock into the metal of the copter until it was mangled. It was the first time he experienced such destructive anger. As if watching another person who was him and yet not him, and he was afraid. But he could not stop; not until the toy copter became a disfigured lump of metal on the ground.

Surprisingly, Mama heard nothing. Perhaps she was cooking, her hearing dulled by the bammy frying in the dutchie. Maybe she was in the backyard washing clothes. Maybe she was pouring out water from the drum into the pan for his evening bath.

When she eventually came onto the veranda, she saw the scraps of the helicopter, lurid bits of red and blue barely visible among the twisted debris. The plastic blades of the propeller were in one corner of the veranda and the rest of the toy was scattered in every direction, while Marcus knelt in the middle looking down at his handiwork. The stone was resting beside him.

He sensed Mama standing in the doorway; he saw her widening eyes; felt her breathing, but there was no sound. The shock of the incomprehensible.

He can't remember Mama punishing him for it. A part of him thinks she must have, but if she did, he can't remember it. She seemed almost childishly sorry, in a way that didn't fit her age, for he'd never known grown-ups to be ever sorry. And she never spoke about the copter again. This was his very first memory. He can still feel the anger. It had never left his body.

Already, at that age, he here felt the frustration of smallness. In the denial of the helicopter he met that feeling, of an animal wanting to break free but not being able to move very far. The beauties and pleasures he had were to be handled sparingly, and not having was the natural order.

All through his life, Marcus would come to know this hedging, this anticipation, this dwelling in smallness. He saw it in the movements of the people in Wanstead, his village, in the way they handled their bodies. This world was moved by powerful people and things they had no grasp on – indescribable forces. Mama had her world. She stayed inside it and so experienced the kind of happiness that comes from being comfortable with your lot. It was a fearful kind of happiness.

He was laughing. He had shared this memory with his friends. There was something comedic about it, though he couldn't articulate what that was. Nobody else seemed to find his story funny. *Ils ont perdu leurs moyens*, he said inwardly; they were thrown.

It was after midnight. Mathilde was looking into the darkened window of the metro carriage opposite her. Agnès cackled oh làlà. The others looked down at their feet, looked around the carriage awkwardly, looked at anything except at Marcus, who could feel the weight of their embarrassment. A weight that was now becoming for him a sort of shame. The shame of silence.

They don't know how to deal with this version of him. They've shut him down by being awkward. Why would he ruin a light-hearted moment by telling this story? But this was his first memory. Somewhere, there was a funny edge to it – he knew it. Perhaps, he thought, too, that the gap between this story of his and his friends' lives also had something funny about it. He wasn't certain what he was thinking. Sure enough, they changed the subject.

Malika Booker was born in London to Guyanese and Grenadian parents. She grew up in Guyana and returned to the UK aged 13, with her parents.

Booker began writing and performing poetry while studying anthropology at Goldsmiths, University of London. She founded the poetry collective Malika's Kitchen, which included Nick Makoha among others. She took part in The Complete Works mentoring programme. Her first collection of poetry, *Pepper Seed*, was published by Peepal Tree Press in 2013, and was shortlisted for the Seamus Heaney Centre prize for best first full collection published in the UK and Ireland. She was the inaugural Poet in Residence at the Royal Shakespeare Company.

Booker's poem "Nine Nights", first published in *The Poetry Review* in autumn 2016, was shortlisted for Best Single Poem in the 2017 Forward Prize.

She has written for radio and for the stage, and her work has appeared in journals and anthologies including *Bittersweet: Contemporary Black Women's Poetry* (1998), *The India International Journal* (2005), *Ten New Poets* (2010), *Out of Bounds, Black & Asian Poets* (2012), and *New Daughters of Africa* (2019).

HOW TINY GOT LUCKY

All she remember from growing up on that plantation was a boy named Joe – same age as she and always skinning his teeth. That boychild always find joke in any situation, no matter what! When she was a little girlchild, all she wanted to do was follow this boy like shadow and play with he all the time. But Joe was one of them children who only content playing with he-self. The more she study him is the more she could think of nothing more compelling than to play with this free-spirited little boy. Even as a young girl on the plantation, she knew life was no joke. All the smiles and laughter get swallowed up by the savagery of everyday life, and Joe the only person in that world who could bring real lightness and laughter to she life.

Well, the day Joe finally allow her to play with him was like something broke, and suddenly he lost all that magic. Was like the laughter fling out of he soul and, just so, he turn simple and ordinary. He turn attainable.

She learnt she lesson well. Is how she got Lucky and kept him, by making a part of herself unreachable, even when they were married.

She knew, as a woman knows her cycle by the moon, that the day she let Lucky know the way he roused her, she would lose him. A sweet man like that had to always thirst and hunger. Something had to be just outside his grasp. He had to know that everything in life don't come easy, especially a woman like she. And like most men, he believed that he was the one who caught her; who made she change she mind, and – wise to the ways of men – she left him to his delusions.

She was a pale woman with freckles all over her face. She could easily pass for white and move over to the other side. But she had grown up on a sugar plantation; she had felt the cruelty of the whip, seen the savagery and the hatred for the black man. Besides, she loved the nigger blood in her, her people, their rhythm, their joviality in the light of so much wickedness. It wasn't even a choice to stay in the skin of the people she felt she belonged to. Never mind them calling her white bitch behind her back. Nobody would dream of bringing that kind of viciousness to her face, they simply wouldn't dare.

She was a tiny woman but she mouth was real real hot. She words could strip you bare; make the biggest, hardest man cry like a child. Make women who came fist forward to fight, turn tail and run.

Lucky always saw her from a distance when he entered her village. He enquired about her and everything he heard about Tiny intrigued him. Soon he began to stride up her street, just to catch a glimpse of this pale, freckle-face, tough-mouth gal. She would not give him a second glance when he passed her on the street. It was like he did not exist – Lucky who never had to work hard for anything or any woman in he whole life. He magnet smile had no effect on this little-piece woman.

She made him tie-tongue and shy like a little knock-kneed schoolboy. When he greeted her, she looked straight through him. He didn't know if he was coming or going with this little piece woman. He had no backup plan. He began to ask he friends for advice and the men were happy to throw talk in his face and behind his back.

"Man, it look like you lose your luck, boy. Tiny have you upside down."

"Look how easy Delilah capture Samson!"

"Nuh is David lick down Goliath backside!"

They joke amongst themselves as if he not there, making him feel stupid. Many of the men had women they were interested in turn off them as soon as Lucky turned up. Davie wife, Jackie, used to have a thing with Lucky, ten years before. Look how long she married Davie and seven years later, she face still turn bright like moon for Lucky. Branman suspect he fiancé, Carol, done slip and fall into Lucky clutches from the way she follow him with she eyes and sometimes share little secret smile with he. Them married man saw their wives craving after Lucky by the underneath glances, the smiles, the forgetfulness, the fluttering whenever his name came up and it burned Davie and Branman and Clifton and Winston – all the men to always be in Lucky's shadow.

So, to see him so confused and stupid over one little woman made them gleeful. They began to love Tiny. She became their champion because Tiny made their lives much easier.

Lucky tried everything to get Tiny's attention. He tried ignoring her back; he tried sweet talking her; he tried leaving presents at her house – a piece of sweet cake, two long sunflower, four gold bracelets and a nice pair of big loop pure gold earrings. Word got to him that she loved hibiscus flowers. He began to leave blood red bouquets outside her door. She would meet him anywhere, look him hard hard in his eye for the longest while, then hand him back his gifts. She never said one word. Wherever she found him, she would stride in and drop the latest gift in front of him, cut she eye and leave.

Lucky did not know what bothered him more, the return of his gifts, the shame of the public returns or the knowledge that he could not stop if he wanted.

He knew Tiny wasn't rich; she taught the school children in her village and gave some private lessons in her house after school. She made a little extra on the side reading the post for the people in her village and writing letters for them. Look at the little board house she lived in begging out for a good lick of paint, and a little fixture work.

When he could take it no more, he lost his mind and walked out into the hardest Guyanese rainfall in years. Rain fat and merciless pelting stinging licks on his skin and Lucky walking in it, thinking hard 'bout this Tiny problem. What really wrong with this woman? Why she making he life so difficult? What he ever do to wrong she? What stubbornness and rudeness she carrying on with? How she behaving like old goat so? Just yesterday, some fellow he ain't even know come up in he business giving advice. "You floundering, buddy. That woman bussing shame in you tail bad and you taking it lying down, man; look at what you doing?"

He walking and he thinking bout all this and the rain busting lash in he ass. Before he know it he was on Miss Tiny street and heading straight up to she door.

And Tiny inside she two-by-four board house that one of her brothers built for her. It had a little kitchen, a dining area, a sitting room and a small bedroom, which fit her bed, her shelves for her little piece of clothes and her big black St James bible with the gold inscription that she kept under her pillow. All she wanted was a lick of blue paint on the outside and some flower-patterned curtains inside to nice it up a bit.

Lucky see Tiny standing under her zinc roof vex, hands on her hips looking up at two holes in she roof where the rain was leaking into her kitchen. She had two big white enamel tin cups under both leaks, but the rain pelting down so hard that the cups filling fast fast and she having to run back and forth to pour it into she bucket.

Just as she was emptying one of the cups in the bucket, Lucky knock she door. She straighten up to see Lucky standing there, soaked, not even a hat on he head and because he not saying nothing, just standing there looking at she, she just opened she mouth and tell him she roof leaking bad in the kitchen.

Lucky turn tail and walk up the road quick time. And Tiny asking sheself, "Why the hell he come out here in all this blasted rain?"

The door knock again and she turn round to see Lucky, dripping wet, holding a hammer, a pan of nails and two sheets of zinc in he hand. Not a word from him.

He point at her ladder lying by the side of the house, walk

over, pick it up and lean it against the side of the house. He climb that roof and start to hammer.

Tiny standing at the bottom, in the rain now, sure the man gone mad, afraid he fall off she roof and break he neck. Because people go say how is she kill he, who, in spite of she bad treatment, still climb her roof in heavy rain to fix she house. Tiny start praying that nothing bad happen to Lucky. When he climb down from the roof, the leaking stop. He fix it just like that. She couldn't leave him outside, so she give him a towel to dry off and a little bush tea with a touch of whisky to prevent him from catching cold.

And is so it began…

ALSO FROM THE READERS AND WRITERS GROUP

Weighted Words
ISBN: 9781845235185; pp. 208; pub. 2021; £9.99

From the colonial idea of 'British' tea; the demasculinising experience of infertility in a Jamaican family; a Black woman being both tourist and tourist attraction on her travels in South Asia, and what it meant to be 'everybody's midwife' in an institutionally racist NHS, through to the experience of an Indian migrant child in the 'country of 'the oppressor' – these are just a few of the themes explored in *Weighted Words* a new anthology by Peepal Tree Press's Readers and Writers Group.

The group comprises writers living in Leeds and West Yorkshire. Through poetry, short stories, confessionals and memoirs, contributors interrogate race, gender, relationship with self and with family, as well as identity in contemporary Britain. Moments of self-reflection sit alongside longer accounts of familial conflicts, personal struggles, and the enduring repercussions of marginalisation.

Edited by Jacob Ross, *Weighted Words* includes the work of established poets like Malika Booker, Khadijah Ibrahiim and Sai Murray alongside previously unpublished writers. Here, a dazzling mix of fresh perspectives and backgrounds mesh and complement each other in a powerful collage of individual experiences, giving rise to a rich and wide-ranging anthology.

ABOUT PEEPAL TREE

Peepal Tree Press has been decolonising bookshelves since 1985, with our focus on Caribbean and Black British writing. We are an independent, specialist publisher supported by the Arts Council of England since 2011 and part of the national portfolio since 2015. In 2024, we established a partnership with HopeRoad Publishing.

Peepal Tree's list is balanced between fiction, poetry and non-fiction, including both academic texts and creative memoirs. We insist our academic titles are accessible to the general reader. By the end of 2024, we will have published 490 books by 320 different authors, including those published in our anthologies. Most of our titles remain in print. Our books have won the Costa Prize, T.S. Eliot, Forward, OCM Bocas, Guyana and Casa de las Americas prizes.

From the beginning, women and LGBTQ+ authors have been fully represented in our lists. We have focused on the new by publishing many first-time authors and have restored to print important Caribbean books in all genres in our Caribbean Classics Series. We have also published overlooked material from the past as a way of challenging received ideas about the Caribbean canon.

As an ACE funded organisation, Peepal Tree supports writer development projects both nationally (Inscribe) and locally (the Readers and Writers Group in Leeds).

We see decolonisation as about overthrowing and repairing an oppressive, economically exploitative and racist power relationship. Many of our books explore the halting, difficult process of overcoming four hundred years of colonialism in the Caribbean in the post-independence period. We see decolonisation as also needing to happen in Britain. We are committed to ending British amnesia over the destructiveness of empire and colonialism, and promoting an understanding of how Britain's long relationship with the Caribbean has contributed to the making of British society in both positive and negative ways. As a publisher, we have taken a stand on supporting Palestinian rights for freedom from a brutal colonial occupation and denial of statehood.

We hope that you enjoyed reading your book as much as we did publishing it. Your purchase directly supports writers to flourish, so thank you. Keep in touch with our newsletter at https://www.peepaltreepress.com/subscribe, discover all our books, and a wealth of other information at www.peepaltreepress.com, and join us on social media @peepaltreepress